Tina◎著

聽懂英文文法

iBT · New TOEIC · IELTS

長難句口語表達

用「聽」的記憶文法，同步「掌握」口語上的長難句表達技巧，
在各大口說測驗「說」得好、立即考到出國入學門檻的分數！

前所未見的兩大學習特色！

超強整合性學習，只要3步驟 100%有效全面提升口說分數！

長難句等同將所傳達的訊息，用一句英文就能完整表達出來，透過❶【熟悉文法概念】▶▶❷【「聽」文法概念結合高分範文】▶▶❸【看文法應用解析、應用】3步驟即刻幫助考生講「對」文法，順暢表達長難句，一次性獲得考官青睞！

隨翻、隨用 的百變長難句句型！

透過熟悉❶【表達個人想法】（開場白）、❷【支持個人想法的理由】（支持的論點）與❸【結論】（結尾句）3大區塊，理出口說測驗的思路與架構，並結合題目，將常用的**句型**、**相關應用**與**論點**做統整性的學習，加深學習印象、還能真正派得上用場！

PREFACE 作者序

口說一向是東亞洲學習者最弱的一環，留學考試更是對我們平常缺乏口語練習的人，特別棘手。因此擁有此書，絕對是掌握了必勝的工具。本書廣收題材，在八章六個單元之中，共選了 48 個重點主題，同時示範了正反論點，並結合於文法學習及藉由套用句型，使讀者到達應用文法句型之學習層次。

十分感謝倍斯特編輯的精心企劃與協助完成此書，同時也感謝我的英國友人－ Kevin Oliver 盡力為我校對以及提供建議。

陳儀眉 (Tina)

EDITOR 編者序

《「聽」懂英文文法和長難句口語表達：應戰 iBT、New TOEIC、IELTS》為什麼要特別強調『長難句』？這是本書的學習特色之一，我們相信，透過連接詞、關係子句、分詞構句等文法技巧可以延伸句子的發展，讓口語表達上跨越單一的主詞＋動詞＋受詞的表達，提升口説的順暢性，也更貼近英語為母語人士的對談，當然也有助於英檢口試上，能有突出的表現，個人優勢即在使用長難句時，一分高下！

其他的學習特色還有：**100% 提升口説分數**：透過 Step 1【熟悉文法概念】、Step 2【「聽」文法概念結合高分範文】、Step 3【看文法應用解析、深入應用補一補】3 步驟，精準講「對」文法，用長難句發表論點也能説得又「好」、又「穩」，給出讓考官驚艷的回答！拉高成績！

百變的長難句句型與延伸應用：透過熟悉『表達個人想法』（開場白）、『支持個人想法的理由』（支持的論點）與『結論』(結尾句）3 大區塊，理出口説測驗的思路與架構，並結合題目，將常用的句型、相關應用與論點做統整性的學習，加深學習印象、還能真正派得上用場！

編輯部敬上

INSTRUCTIONS
學習特色與使用說明

單元主題、應用句型，搭配口配口說主題，要學什麼，哪些是重點，一看就知道！

由『重點文法搶先看』，立即鎖定單元重點文法，並從『重要句型與文法放大鏡』，放大檢視要學的文法！

2-1
私立學校和公立學校之利弊

| 應用句型 |
It is well-known that ...／眾所皆知……

| 搭配口說主題 |
私立學校和公立學校之利弊

重點文法搶先看

① 被動語態
② It's well-known that...（眾所皆知的……）

重要句型與文法放大鏡

① 被動語態：被動語態的目的是強調動詞的接受者，
詞，或者是不知動作者（也就是主詞）時用被動語
之外，應盡量少使用被動語態。方法是主詞與受
調，解析如下：
句型：
★ 主動：主詞 A＋一般動詞＋受詞 B
★ 被動：主詞 B＋be＋Vpp.＋（介系詞＋受詞 A）
提點（Vpp. 指過去分詞）（通常為：by~）。
位置對調時，除了本身需做變化（例：I→b

50

文法和口說應用大結合

以上文法和句型可以運用到 IBT、NEW TOEIC 及 IELTS 考試上面，以下列的題目舉例 Track 07

People want the best education for themselves or their children. There is much debate about private schools and public/state schools. What are the advantages and disadvantages of these two types of schools?

人們都想自己或自己的孩子受最好的教育。關於私立學校和公立學校有許多爭論。這兩類學校的優勢和劣勢是什麼？

高分範文

Well, let me start with private schools. Firstly, I will talk about class sizes. They tend to be smaller at private schools, and therefore, private schools usually have better teacher-student ratios. The benefits coming from those schools are that pupils gain much greater attention from teachers. As a result, students' particular

好的，讓我先從私立學校開始。首先，我會談班級大小。私立學校的傾向是比較小的班級。因此，私立學校通常有較好的師生比。這些學校的好處就是中小學生可以得到老師更多的注意力。結果，學生在學業上有特別的需要

52

看相關類型的題目都問些什麼，並搭配高分範文，中英對照、單字套色，關鍵句型輔以底線，邊聽 MP3 邊學，提升學習性與臨場感！

高分範文的回答兼具正反面論點，關鍵句型則會在『文法應用解析』另作更深入的分析、應用，有助論點建構，更加熟悉句型的用法！

academic needs and weaknesses are easier to be noticed by teachers. On the other hand, it is well known that their tuition fees are hugely expensive, which is the major drawback.

或是弱點都可以比較容易被老師注意到。在另一方面，眾所周知的是他們巨量昂貴的學費，這就是最大的缺點。

In contrast, public schools are more affordable, and generally speaking, public school teachers are more highly qualified than private school teachers. If public schools can acquire enough funding from the government, they can have more access to resources and technology than private schools which cannot acquire sufficient funding. The disadvantages come from their larger class sizes. Pupils get less attention from teachers, and this results in disappointment by parents. So my conclusion is, I

對照之下，公立學校比較付得起，而且一般而言，公立學校老師比私立學校老師合格很多。如果公立學校可以從政府那得到足夠的經費，他們可以有更多的機會得到比無法獲得足夠經費的私立學校更多資源和科技。而他們較多的班級中小學生會獲得少的注意力，這家長的不滿意是，有天份和聰子在任何學校都

CHAPTER 1 媒體－基本句型 1
2 教育－基本句型 2
3 環境、交通

貼心的書側索引，呼應學習內容，方便查找，加深學習印象！

believe a gifted and intelligent child can thrive and succeed in any school, while a less intelligent child may benefit from the extra academic attention at private school. Parents and students should gather sufficient information about the school in order to make an informed choice.

勃發展，而較不聰明的孩子可以在私立學校，因為學業上受到特別的重視而獲益。我相信父母和學生應該收集關於學校足夠的資訊，以作出充份的選擇。

關鍵單字解密

1. teacher-student ratio *n.* 師生比	2. As a result *ph.* 結果
3. academic *adj.* 學業上的、學術的	4. drawback *n.* 缺點

『關鍵單字解密』蒐羅高分範文內的重點字彙，有助即刻複習，拉高學習效率！噢，別忘了，口試時要避免使用罕見字，以免用得不順，造成反效果！

INSTRUCTIONS 學習特色與使用說明

進入『文法應用解析、深入應用補一補』，跟著老師剖析高分範文的高分句型、論點！

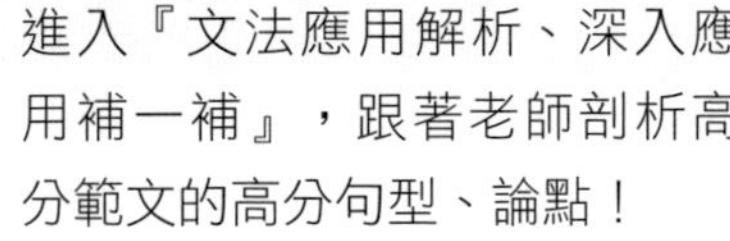

文法應用解析、深入應用補一補
❶ ... pupils can gain much greater attention from teachers. As a result, students' particular academic needs and weaknesses are easier to be noticed by teachers.

解析淺顯易懂，馬上就能看到重點！

2-1 | 私立學校和公立學校之利弊

解析

"As a result, …"（結果/因此，…）是連接因果的重要句型，前句是因，句型：因句… **As a result,** 果句。

其它應用

Students acquire promptly support from their te… As a result, they made progress on their ac… performance.（他們獲得老師的立即支持。因此，他…業表現上有進步。）

❷ ... a gifted and intelligent child can thrive and s… in any school, while a less intelligent child may … from the extra academic attention at private scho…

解析

while 是用來對照在比較的兩者之間的不同之處，中文…作「而」，也可以翻成這兩個字原本的意思－「當」…在比較）。句型：**A 子句，while B 子句**.

其它應用

Small class sizes can improve discipline, wh… harder for teachers to maintain control of a larger…（小規模的班級可以改善紀律，而較大的班級使老師…

在入門篇 **Part 1_Chapter 4** 以及進階篇 **Part 2_Chapter 8**，每單元的句型整理與應用，是在短時間必須上場應試考生們的好幫手！

4-2
風俗文化

| 以下列的題目舉例 |

- **Talk about your culture. What's unique about it?** 談論你們的文化。有什麼獨特之處？
- **What are the advantages and disadvantages of private schools and public/state schools?** 私立學校和公立學校的優勢和劣勢（Ch2 2-1）
- **Describe your hometown/country: today and the past.** 請談談你的家鄉／國家：現在與過去（Ch3 3-1）
- **Current environmental issues and solutions** 現在的環境問題和解決方案（Ch3 3-3）

❶ **要求作兩者之間比較，以：**"Well, let me start with…" or "to start with,…" 開始。

解析 1 談文化經常要作比較，當你被要求作兩者之間比較，你可以由："Well, let me start with…" 開始。well 是發語詞，"Let me….''是祈使句，祈使句是表示請求、命令、勸告或禁止等語氣的句子。由於此類句型都是用來跟眼前的人（You）說話，所以通常省略主詞，You。因為原本的句型中的主詞是第二人稱，所以動詞也就是同原形動詞。"Well, let me start with…"就是「好的，讓我先……」。

128

其他應用將高分句型，以該單元的口說題目為主軸，做造句、應用，加深對句型的印象，擴增論述的資料庫！

看題目立即了解可能的考題，除收錄新題外，也有先前單元出現的題目，預習、複習好都好用！

句型列點式整理，從第一段的開頭句、表明因果句，到結尾句等，都有精確的解析！

❸ **表明因果的重要說法**：As a result, as a consequence

解析 3 as a result, as a consequence 介詞片語做副詞，翻作「結果」、「因此」，用以連接句意上的前一句因，而後一句是果。

應用 3.1 As a result, students' particular academic needs and weaknesses are easier noticed by teachers. (Ch2 2-1)（結果，學生在學業上有特別的需要或是弱點，都可以比較容易被老師注意到。《節選自 Ch2 2-1》）

應用 3.2 The cultural preference of male descendants was dominant. As a consequence, parents preferred a boy to a girl.（在過去在文化上偏好男性子孫是主法。因此，家長們偏好男孩，而不是女孩。）

應用 3.3 In 1895, China was defeated in the Japanese War. As a consequence, Taiwan was to Japan and colonised for 50 years.（在 1895 在中日戰爭戰敗；結果，台灣就被割讓給日本，並殖民五十年。）

應用的第一句整理出先前單元的句子，有助複習論述；延伸應用則能看到其他不同的論述，『句型』＋『論述』多重複習提升學習效率！

❹ **作比較的重要說法**：In contrast, in comparison to, unlike

解析 4 In contrast, in comparison to, unlike 都是「對照之下」、「與……成對比」，都是用來對比兩件事或兩個人之不同處。

應用 4.1 ... it is well known that their tuition fees are hugely expensive, which is the major drawback. In contrast, public schools are more affordable,... (Ch2 2-1)（眾所周知的是他們巨量昂貴的學費，這就是最大的缺點。對照之下，公立學校比較付得起⋯⋯《節選自 Ch2 2-1》）

*此例是作 private school 和 public schools 兩者之間的比較

應用 4.2 In comparison to the past, the birth rate in Taiwan has reduced steadily. Increased education and delayed marriages reduce the potential of females aged between 20 and 30 to become a mother.（與過去作比較，台灣的出生率已經穩定的下降。教育提高和晚婚減少 20 至 30 歲的女士成為母親的可能性。）

*此例是作 the past 和 now（由 has reduced 知道）兩者之間的比較

搶先看『句型』＋『論述』的應用！

CONTENTS 目次

PART 1 >> 入門篇

CHAPTER 1 媒體–基本句型 1

CHAPTER 2 教育–基本句型 2

CHAPTER 3 環境、交通–連接詞

CHAPTER 4 重要句型、搭配主題、思考關鍵字整理

2 PART >> 進階篇

CHAPTER 5 社交－連接詞、詞性轉換、時態

CHAPTER 6 價值觀－名詞子句、關係代名詞、邏輯

CHAPTER 7 生活旅遊、政府政策－分詞構句

CHAPTER 8 重要句型、搭配主題、思考關鍵字整理

將看完的單元打個勾，提升口說自信心！

☐ 看完 Chapter 1、2 基本句型、媒體、教育類題型沒問題！

☐ 搞定 Chapter 3 連接詞用法、環境、交通類題型都會了！

☐ 複習 Chapter 4 前3章總整理與延伸應用，學習印象更深了！

各類英文檢定考試的口說評分項目不離以下三點

第一｜用字準確 (accuracy)、第二｜句型變化 (variation)、第三｜論點 (concrete supporting ideas)，Part 1 入門篇先教你正確句型，並教你套用在論點應用上。同時以最常見的口說題目作切入，一邊熟悉文法、句型，一邊練習口說，讓口說上的用字、論點又準、又好！

1-1 兒童上網問題

| 應用句型 |
I agree. / I don't agree.
我同意……／我不同意……

| 搭配口說主題 |
兒童上網問題

重點文法搶先看

① 主詞（S）＋不及物動詞（Vi.）

② 主詞（S）＋及物動詞（Vt.）＋受詞（O）

重要句型與文法放大鏡

① 主詞（S）＋不及物動詞（Vi.）

英文中**只有**五大基本句型。也就是說所有的英文句子都能歸類於這五種之一。第一基本句型即是主詞加不及物動詞，「物」，就是受詞的意思，顧名思義，「不及物動詞」就是後面不接受詞的動詞，句子中只要有這兩個元素：主詞和不及物動詞，除了在文法上它是正確的句子，就語意而言，也是完整的句子。例如：我同意 I agree.、我不同意 I disagree.，是文法上和語意都完整的句子。（對！句子很短，他們英文也有簡單的啦！哈哈！）

其他的例子還有：Money talks.（金錢萬能）、Time flies.（時光飛逝）。這些句子都可以加上修飾語，如：I totally agree. 我完全同意。我們也可以將 I agree. 說得再具體些，如：我同意你：I agree with you. 此時要加上介系詞 —— with。

注意介系詞的不同：

★ S＋agree with 人

★ S＋agree to 事／to do sth.（sth.= something）

agree 後面還可以加名詞子句（**一個動詞有多重身份並不奇怪**）例如：I agree that the Internet is very useful.（我同意網路非常有用。）這句的句型就成了主詞加及物動詞加受詞，也就是第二大基本句型，解析如下：

② **主詞（S）＋及物動詞（Vt.）＋受詞（O.）**

「及物動詞」（Vi.）就是後面必須要接受詞的動詞。及物動詞就是後面要接受詞才能讓語意完整。給一個最簡單的例子：I love you.（我愛你。）。試想 I love. 這句話是不是沒有說完的感覺呢？其他的例子還有：The children abandoned learning from printed books.（這些孩子們放棄了從紙本書籍學習。）

文法和口說應用大結合

以上文法和句型可以運用到 IBT、NEW TOEIC 及 IELTS 考試上面，以下列的題目舉例 Track 01

There has been a tendency that children start going on the Internet at younger ages. Some people think it is a good trend. Do you agree or disagree? Explain why.

小孩越來越早開始上網已經成為一個趨勢。有人認為這是一個好的趨勢。你同意或是不同意？請解釋理由。

高分範文

I don't agree. Personally, I don't like children to use the Internet at a very young age, say, under seven. The main reason is that paper books would be forgotten and abandoned by children because they may be far less attractive to them. It would be dangerous if virtual materials replace printed books.

我個人認為，我不喜歡小孩在很小的時候，像是小於七歲，開始使用網路。主要的原因是紙本書籍可能會被小孩遺忘或是遺棄，因為它們可能很不吸引孩子。如果虛擬的材料取代印刷的書籍，這將會是一件危險的事情。

First of all, children would lose interest in learning from paper books when they are obsessed by the abundant sound and visual effects of online materials. If this were the case, they would lose the opportunities to learn from these printed materials.

首先，當孩子們著迷于網路材料豐富的聲光效果時，他們會失去從紙本書籍上學習的興趣。如果這是事實的話，他們將失去從這些印刷材料中學習的機會。

Second, prolonged spending time on the computer or other electronic devices deteriorates eye sight. Third, the information is not always true on the Net. Besides, there are always some improper advertisements popping up. These are some of the reasons that I don't agree children should use the Internet when they are too young.

第二，經久花時間在電腦或是其他的電子設備上會損害視力。第三，在網路上的訊息並不總是真實的。此外，總是會有一些不合適的廣告跳出來。這些是我不贊成小孩在太早的年紀使用網路的原因。

關鍵單字解密

1. abandon *v.* 放棄	2. virtual *adj.* 虛擬的
3. obsess *v.* 使著迷	4. abundant *adj.* 豐富的
5. prolonged *adj* 冗長的	6. deteriorate *v.* 惡化

文法應用解析、深入應用補一補

❶ Personally, I don't like children to use the internet at a very young age, say, under seven.

解析

托福、雅思考題不可免的，常常要問你個人的想法。除了用"I think…" 之外，還可以 Personally 的片語來表示：Personally,… 後面直接接你的論點。

其它應用 1

Personally, it is beneficial for children to learn how to use the computer.（就個人而言，孩子們學習如何使用電腦是有益的。）

其它應用 2

表示「我個人認為……」還可以用以下的片語來表示：Personally speaking, I suppose…= In my opinion, 後面直接接你的論點。**提點** Personally speaking 合起來就是以我個人而言…、以我個人來說…、以我之見…，也是表達個人的意見。suppose 是假想，設想也是認為的意思。

例 Personally speaking, I suppose the vast of knowledge can be gained just with a touch of a finger.（以我之見，我認為廣大的知識在指間一觸即得。）

❷ Besides, there are always some improper advertisements popping up.

解析

在提供更多的理由和補充說法時，可以用以下的單字或片語：Besides,... = In addition,... = Additionally,... = Moreover, 你的論點。

其它應用

Besides, children can learn to be an independent learner through searching for information on their own.（此外，孩子可以經由自己搜尋資料而成為獨立的學習者。）

1-2 媒體報導的滿意度（公正性、真實性，以及客觀性之批判）

｜應用句型｜
I find it especially true／我發現（某事）非常真實……

｜搭配口說主題｜
媒體報導的滿意度

重點文法搶先看

① 主詞（S）＋連綴動詞（V）＋補語（SC）

② 主詞（S）＋動詞（V）＋受詞（O）＋補語（OC）

重要句型與文法放大鏡

這個單元主要的文法是討論另外兩大基本句型。現在看一個簡單的句子：It is interesting.（它很有趣）。interesting 是形容詞，在這裡做就是作主詞補語；主詞補語是什麼意思呢？就是補充說明主詞。如果我們只有前半部——It is... 你會發現這個句子並不完整，所以就需要主詞補語使句子完整。它的句型結構可以寫成：

① 主詞（S）＋連綴動詞（V）＋主詞補語（SC）

主要是配合連綴動詞，連綴動詞一般有：be 動詞，

seem、appear、become、feel、look、sound、keep、maintain 再看更多的句子：

例 1 Their reports seem objective.（他們的報導似乎很客觀。）**例 2** With the rise of social media, sharing opinions has become easy.（隨著社會媒體的崛起，分享意見變得更簡單了。）**提點** 現在我們比較這個句子：I find it interesting. interesting 在這裡不是主詞補語了，因為它不是補充説明主詞，它是補充説明一件事情（受詞），是怎麼樣的呢？是很有趣的。這句話的結構就是第二點：

② **主詞（S）＋動詞（V）＋受詞（O）＋受詞補語（OC）.**

這裡的動詞是「不完全動詞」（名稱不重要），它需要補語才能表示完整的意思。看以下這句話：**例 1** People say that every newspaper has its own political agenda. I find **it（受詞）**especially **true（受詞補語）**in my country. **提點** 人們説每家報紙都有他們自己的政治立場。我發現這在我的國家這是更是如此。it 是指前面那句話，政治立場的事情。I find.（我發現。）這句子並沒有講完，發現它（受詞）是怎麼樣的呢？是確有其事的，句子才完整。

文法和口說應用大結合

以上文法和句型可以運用到 IBT、NEW TOEIC 及 IELTS 考試上面，以下列的題目舉例 Track 02

Are you satisfied with the quality of the media or news reporting?

你對於媒體或新聞報導的品質滿意嗎？

高分範文

In my opinion, I would say that every newspaper has its own **political agenda**. I find it especially true in my country. Each Taiwanese newspaper is in favour of one political party. They criticize the opposite party in a **biased** way and in a very obvious **manner**. The public have the right to know the truth. However, they can't because every newspaper is biased, and makes public their unjust

以我之見，我會說每家報紙都有自己的政治目的。我發現這在我的國家更是如此。每一家台灣報紙都偏好一個政黨。他們以非常明顯的方式偏頗反對黨。大眾有知的權利，然而，他們無法得到，因為每家報社都是偏頗的，公開的是他們不公正的言論。他們誤導讀者。

opinions. They mislead readers.

I am also not happy about the content of social pages. Their content is too selective; they choose what they think may please the majority of readers. These are my opinions about the traditional media of newspapers.

我對社會版的內容也不高興。他們的內容太選擇性了。他們選擇他們認為會取悅大眾讀者的內容。這是我關於傳統的報紙媒體的意見。

Now I'd like to comment on the social media such as bloggers or Twitter. You should be more careful about them. They are usually full of personal opinions, not based on facts. You should be careful not to be misled by them.

現在我想要批評社交媒體，像是部落格或是推特。你必須對它們更小心。它們通常充斥個人意見，而非基於事實。你必須非常小心以免被它們誤導。

關鍵單字解密

1. political agenda *ph.* 政治目的	2. biased *adj.* 偏頗的
3. manner *n.* 樣子、方式	4. comment on *ph.v.* 批評
5. base on *ph. v.* 基於	6. be misled *ph.* 被誤導

文法應用解析、深入應用補一補

❶ Each Taiwanese newspaper is in favour of one political party.

解析

in favour of 偏好，是介系詞片語，通常與 be 動詞連用，後面接名詞，如果沒有名詞，只有動詞，要用動名詞（動詞＋ing）

其它應用 1

Comparing social media with traditional media, I am in favour of social media because I can put whatever I want to say on the website. In the past, opinion was filtered by traditional media.（傳統媒體相比，我偏好社交媒體，因為我可以在網站上隨所欲言。在過去，言論會被傳統媒體過濾。）

其它應用 2

I am in favour of traditional media; you can check the integrity of news stories easier because there are fewer sources, unlike social media, where you would be lost in the sea of different versions of the stories.（我偏好傳統媒體；我偏好傳統媒體；你可以較容易檢查新聞報導的公正性，因為來源較少不像社交媒體，你可能會迷失在不同版本的故事的大海中。）

② I am also not happy about the content on social pages.

解析

“happy” 快樂這一個字，同學可能會誤會是很不正式的，但是老師也是到英國才了解這個字很普遍，而且也會用在很正式的場合。比如說他們常常會問：“Are you happy for me to do this for you? ” 表示「你願意我做什麼什麼事情嗎？」或「我可以做……嗎」？

其它應用

I am happy to see the rise of social media because opinion can get through as front page journalism.（我很樂意見到社會媒體的崛起，因為意見可以如同頭版新聞一般散播。）

1-3 媒體產生的問題

｜應用句型｜
give sb. sth.
／給（某人）某物

｜搭配口說主題｜
媒體的問題

重點文法搶先看

① 主詞（S）＋授與動詞（V）＋間接受詞（IO）＋直接受詞（DO）

② 主詞（S）＋授與動詞（V）＋直接受詞（DO）＋介系詞＋間接受詞（IO）

重要句型與文法放大鏡

① 這個單元主要的文法是討論第五種基本句型：主詞＋動詞＋間接受詞＋直接受詞。這種和第二種基本句型（1-1）都是「主詞＋動詞＋受詞」，差別是這種比第二種多了一個受詞，原因是這類型的動詞——授與動詞，必須牽涉到兩個人事物。**間接受詞通常是人，直接受詞通常是物，現在看一個簡單的句子：**

例 1 He gave me some money.

解析 give/gave 是授與動詞，me 是間接受詞，some money 是直接受詞。再看更多的句子：The media should give（動詞）the public（間接受詞）the right to know the truth（直接受詞）.（媒體應該給大眾知的權利。）我們也可以這樣說：The media should give（動詞）the right to know the truth（直接受詞）to the public（間接受詞）.

② 直接受詞若是放在間接受詞的前面，需要有介系詞 to 或 for 隔開兩個受詞，使用 to 或 for 依動詞而定。

A. **使用介系詞 to 的動詞，句型公式：** 主詞＋授與動詞＋直接受詞＋to＋間接受詞 ：give、hand、pass、offer、allow、cause、lend、owe、pay、promise、sell、send、show、take、tell、write、read、teach 如上例句。

B. 使用介系詞 for 的授與動詞，句型公式： 主詞＋授與動詞＋直接受詞＋for＋間接受詞 ：leave, buy, choose, cook, find, get, fetch, save, pick, make, reserve, order

例 The Paparazzi should leave some private room for celebrities.（狗仔應該留給名人一些私人的空間。）

文法和口說應用大結合

以上文法和句型可以運用到 IBT、NEW TOEIC 及 IELTS 考試上面，以下列的題目舉例 Track 03

It is often said that people have the right to know. Everything about celebrities is always interesting to the public. Gradually, there has been a growth of the paparazzi. Some feel that the paparazzi invades celebrities' privacy. What do you feel about the paparazzi's behaviors?

人有知的權利。大眾對於名人的所有事情，總是很感興趣。逐漸地產生了狗仔文化。一些人認為狗仔隊侵犯了名人的隱私。你對狗仔隊的行為看法是如何？

高分範文

It is true that people have the right to know. Nevertheless, nobody's privacy should be deprived just because their lives are interesting to other people. The Paparazzi do not have the right to invade celebrities' personal space.

的確人們有知的權利。然而，沒有人的隱私可以被剝奪，只因為別人對他們的生活感興趣。狗仔沒有侵犯名人私人空間的權利。

They follow famous people everywhere in order to take photos for money. They intrude into their personal lives and disturb them when they try to enjoy family or social life. I saw news regarding some celebrities who were suffering from depression or committed suicide because of too much pressure from the paparazzi, the photos and news they spread. They ruin celebrities' lives just for profit.

為了要拍照賣錢，他們到處跟蹤名人。他們侵入他們的私人生活，在他們享受家庭和社交生活的時候打擾他們。我看過關於一些名人因為太多來自於狗仔隊散佈照片和新聞的壓力，而蒙受憂鬱症之苦或是自殺。他們毀了名人的生活，只為了利益。

On the other hand, they flourish because people actually care too much about celebrities' lives. Put yourself in their shoes, would you accept being 'paparazzied'? Therefore, I suggest that not only should they be forbidden, but also the public should care far less about celebrities' lives.

在另一方面，他們會興盛是因為人們太關心名人的生活。設身處地的想，你會接受被狗仔跟拍嗎？因此我建議他們必須被禁止，而社會大眾也必須減少關心名人的生活。

關鍵單字解密

1. nevertheless *adv.* 然而	2. invade *v.* 侵犯
3. regarding *prep.* 關於	4. suffer *v.* 蒙受
5. depression *n.* 憂鬱症	6. commit suicide *ph.v.* 自殺
7. ruin *v.* 破壞，毀壞	

文法應用解析、深入應用補一補

❶ Nobody's privacy should be deprived just because their lives are interesting to other people.

解析

interesting 是「令人覺得有趣的」，是情緒動詞－interest 加 ing（Ving），是現在分詞作形容詞用，表心情令人……的。現在分詞基本上後面加介系詞 to。interested 是「感到有興趣的」，是過去分詞表感到……的，是情緒動詞用完成式過去分詞（Vpp）的型態。後面的介系詞用 in。現在比較這兩種分詞的句型：

★ 某人／事 be interesting to A 某.（某人／事令 A 某覺得有趣。）

★ A 某 be interested in 某人／事.（A 某對某人／事感到有興趣。）

其它應用 1

Celebrities' lives are often interesting to people.（名人的生活通常令人覺得有趣。）

其它應用 2

The Paparazzi are interested in making a profit, regardless of ruining the lives of celebrities.（狗仔隊對賺錢感到興趣，而不管毀了名人的生活。）

❷ On the other hand, they flourish because people actually care too much about celebrities' lives.

解析

On the other hand,是對同一件事物，提供不同角度或看法，所以之前你已經說過一種看法，之前的可以用 "on one hand," 切入。

其它應用

On one hand, I am a peace-lover. On the other hand, I feel happy when I see some celebrity attack the paparazzi because in a lot of cases, they ask for it.（一方面，我是一個和平愛好者。但另一方面，當我看到一些名人攻擊狗仔隊，我感到高興，因為很多情況下，他們是自找的。）**提點** "On one hand,", "On the other hand," 可以同時用。

1-4 媒體輿論

| 應用句型 |
Not only ... , but also.../ 不僅……，也是……

| 搭配口說主題 |
媒體輿論

重點文法搶先看

① 表示地點或方向的副詞開頭

② 具有限制或否定意義的副詞包括：Little/Rarely、not only...(but) also、Only when 的倒裝句

重要句型與文法放大鏡

基本句型只有五種，再複雜的句子也是以上五種基本句型衍伸來的。句子可以加很多形容詞也可以加很多副詞，或是合併很多個句子，但是最本質的一個主詞一個主要動詞還是不變。每一個句子基本上符合這五種基本句型，特殊句型是以上五種基本句型的變形，如祈使句、倒裝句。

① **當句子用以標示地點或方向的副詞開頭，例如：here、there、up、down、in、out、away、round、over、back**

動詞要放到主詞前面，除非主詞是代名詞。例：Here come some paparazzi.（有狗仔隊過來了。）提點 comes 動詞 some paparazzi 主詞，地點副詞 here 開頭，動詞要放到主詞前面，形成倒裝句。

② 具有限制或否定意義的副詞包括：little, seldom, rarely, hardly, scarcely, never, not only... (but) also, only then, only by, only when, … 等等。副詞放句首，後面接助動詞或 be 動詞，形成倒裝句。以下介紹三組字詞：

1. Little/Rarely：People's voices are rarely heard by politicians in some countries.（人民的聲音在一些國家很少被政治人物所聽到。）
2. not only... (but) also... 不僅……而且（也）……："but" 可以省略。例 With the Internet network, opinion can be expressed not only more conveniently, but also faster.（有著（因為）網路，意見不但可以表達的更方便，也更快。）提點 記住這一組片語：不僅…而且…要用對稱結構，也就是說這兩個詞的後面接的詞，詞性要一致。
3. Only when…＋S＋V＋倒裝句：Only when politicians lose their votes do they realize that public opinion plays a crucial role.（只有當政客流失他們的選票時，他們才會了解輿論扮演著重要的角色。）

 文法和口說應用大結合

以上文法和句型可以運用到 IBT、NEW TOEIC 及 IELTS 考試上面，以下列的題目舉例 Track 04

Do you enjoy there being a media to upload public opinion or do you think it is not necessary? 或是

Is public opinion necessary? Do you think public opinion can inform the government's decision-making? 你喜歡媒體可以上載輿論？或是你認為輿論有必要嗎？你認為輿論可以作為政府決策作之參考嗎？

 高分範文

In my opinion, public opinion is necessary because people should be allowed to express their ideas on any particular issue, problem, etc. Hopefully it can be a guide to decision-makers, if they are smart enough.

以我之見，輿論是必須的。因為人們需要被允許表達他們對於一個特定的議題、問題等等的想法。希望它可以指引政策決定者，如果政客夠聰明的話。

For decision-makers, public opinion represents a common or popular opinion on a particular

對於政策決定者來說，輿論呈現對一個特定的問題的一般和大眾

issue, and thus provides them with a guide for action, decisions, or the like. It's particularly important for politicians to pay attention to public opinion in a democratic country.

的看法，以提供他們對其行動、決策和其他等的指引。關注輿論對在民主國家政策的決定者是特別重要。

However, the impact is not always positive. First of all, it is often the case that public opinion is ambivalent, and thus isn't helpful to guide the government. Secondly, with online media, public opinion can be expressed more conveniently, spread faster, and can be interactive. These are advantages which traditional media cannot be compared with. However, the network is like a sharp "double-edged sword"; spreading disinformation or rumors on the Internet is not only much easier than in reality, but also more difficult to trace the source.

然而其影響不全然是正面的。首先，輿論常常是模擬兩可的，因此對於指導政府就不太能夠有幫助。其二，以網路媒體，輿論可以被傳播的更方便，散佈地更快，而且能夠互動。這些好處是傳統的媒體無法可比擬的。但是，網路就像是一把兩刃刀；在網路上散佈不實訊息和造謠，不僅是比在現實生活中更簡單，而且也很難去追蹤其來源。

關鍵單字解密

1. be allowed to *ph.* 被允許	2. hopefully *adv.* 希望地
3. decision-makers *n.* 政策決定者	4. democratic *adj.* 民主的
5. ambivalent *adj.* 模擬兩可的	6. spread *v.* 散佈
7. disinformation *n.* 不實訊息	

文法應用解析、深入應用補一補

❶ It is often the case that public opinion is ambivalent.

解析

case 是情形，例子，常常是這種情形，或是這種例子是常見的。後面接詞 that 子句。也可以先把事情描述在前，再用形容詞子句 which is often the case。

其它應用

It is often the case that the Network is like a sharp "double-edged sword". On one hand, it provides a convenient way for the public to express their ideas; on the other hand, it can be used as a tool to disseminate false information.（網路就像銳利的兩刃刀，是常有的情形。在一方面，它提供了一個很方便的方式給大眾表達他們的想法。另一方面，它可以作為散佈假訊息的工具。）

❷ Spreading disinformation or rumors on the Internet is not only much easier than in reality but also difficult to trace

解析

Ving 作主詞。Spreading 是 "Spread" 動詞加上 ing，來的形式。成 ving 動名詞。為什麼需要動名詞？因為一個句子只能有一個動詞的原則。句子中只要提到第二個動詞，就必須把它變成動名詞或不定詞。動名詞不再算是動詞，而是具有名詞的作用：可作主詞、受詞、補語。此例是作主詞。常常可以與不定詞（to V）替代使用。

其它應用

Controlling disinformation and rumors circulated within a society is necessary.（控制在社會當中所散佈的不實訊息和謠言是必須的。）提點 單一項的不定詞，動名詞當主詞算單數，要配合用單數動詞。**此例比較適合用虛主詞構句，避免頭重腳輕，虛主詞構句將會在** Ch1 1-6 **當中詳解**。

1-5 媒體管制

｜應用句型｜
I would say...／
我會這麼說⋯⋯

｜搭配口說主題｜
媒體管制

重點文法搶先看

① 沒有詞義的助動詞

② 情態助動詞

重要句型與文法放大鏡

助動詞有二大類：本身沒有詞義的助動詞，及有詞義的情態助動詞。

① **本身沒有詞義的助動詞**，它是用來幫助主要動詞形成各種時態、語氣、語態、疑問句、或否定句。最常使用的助動詞有 do (do, does, did)；Be 動詞 (am, are, is, was, were, be, being, been) 和 have (have, has, had)

② **情態助動詞**用來表示：可能性、必須、允許、義務、禁止或

能力。常見的情態助動詞有：will, would, shall, should, can, could, may, might, must, ought to 等，放在主要動詞之前。其他補充有……

★ 在表達意見時，常會表示到推測，用來表示推測的可能性的情態助動詞有：will; can; may，而這些情態助動詞的過去式形式，正好用來表示推測的可能性較低，它們的過去式形式分別為：would/could/ might。但，用過去式形式也可用來表示委婉、客氣 (hedging)，尤其是在正式的寫作上。所以我會用：In my opinion, I would say... ., 而非：I will say... .

★ 其它例句：I would say (that) porn ads. should be forbidden. 我會說色情廣告應該被禁止。（ads. = advertisement; 廣告）**提點** that 在這裡因為當受詞的連接詞，所以可以省略。此句不用 can/could 是因它們表示能力，不符合句意。表示義務或建議用 should; ought to。

★ may/might 特別指事情有可能發生

例 Porn ads. may disturb children and teenagers, and cause a negative impact on them.（色情廣告很可能會擾亂兒童和青少年，並且對其造成負面的影響。）

文法和口說應用大結合

以上文法和句型可以運用到 IBT、NEW TOEIC 及 IELTS 考試上面，以下列的題目舉例 Track 05

Some people think governments should give complete freedom to the media. Others think governments should implement or enhance censorship on the media. What do you think? Explain why.

一些人認為政府應該給媒體完全的自由。而一些人認為政府應該設立或加強媒體的審查制度。你認為呢？請解釋理由。

高分範文

Personally, I would say our government should increase censorship on the media. Today, when you turn on your TV or flip over your newspaper, you are flooded with **commercials** or advertisements. To me, many of these seem too **exaggerated**. However, you never know the appealing words used in

就個人而言，我會說政府應該對媒體審查。今天當你打開電視或是翻開你的報紙，你會被商業廣告所淹沒。其中很多，對我來說，似乎都太誇張了。而直到你買的他們的產品之後，你才會知道這些使用在商業廣告中吸引人

commercials or advertisements are not true until you buy their products. Then you feel frustrated and deceived after paying so much money. Who gives the merchants the right to "tell lies" in public and deceive the public?

的文字不是真的。然後，在付了太多錢之後，你就會覺得沮喪被騙。是誰給這些商人公開說謊欺騙大眾的權利呢？

This is not right. The government should implement some regulations on commercials and increase censorship. They should take the initiative to inspect false advertising in order to protect consumers' rights. Moreover, not only should commercial advertisements be governed, but governments also examine other media, such as news reports, books, TV and films to block false or objectionable content.

這樣是不對的。政府應該建立一些對於廣告商業的管制，並且加強審查。他們應該主動來檢查不實廣告，以保護消費者的權力。更者，不僅是商業廣告，政府也應該檢視其他的媒體，像是新聞報導、書籍、電視和電影阻絕假的、令人反感的內容。

關鍵單字解密

1. commercial *n.* 商業廣告	2. exaggerated *adj.* 誇張
3. appealing *adj.* 吸引人的	4. deceived *v.pp.* 被騙
5. merchant *n.* 商人	6. objectionable *adj.* 令人反感的

文法應用解析、深入應用補一補

❶ You never know these appealing words used in commercials or advertisements are not true until you buy their products.

解析

until（直到……才……）表時間的副詞子句的連接詞，連接兩個事件，事件 A 和事件 B。以下句型：**事件 A** until **事件 B.** 表直到事件 B 出現時，事件 A 才結束

其它應用 1

I thought the product was amazing until I bought it.（我一直認為這個產品是很棒的，一直到我買了它。）提點 前面為事件 A，前面為事件 B；也就是，我一直相信這個產品是很棒的，一直到我買了它才結束這個想法（就是買錯了 ☹）

其它應用 2

Governments should establish censorship on the media until it is too late.（政府應該在為時已晚之前，對媒體建立審查制度。）

❷ The government **should** implement some regulations on commercials and enhance censorship.

解析

should 是情態助動詞，後面必須接原形動詞（V）。shouldn't 表示「不應該」。

其它應用 1

Governments **should** take the initiative in inspecting the media.（政府應該對於檢視媒體採取主動。）

其它應用 2

The government **shouldn't** spread some information that cause social chaos.（政府不應該散布可能會造成社會動盪的信息。）

1-6 電影分級制度的看法

| 應用句型 |
It is necessary to...／（某事）有其必要……

| 搭配口說主題 |
電影分級制度的看法

重點文法搶先看

① 關於虛主詞

重要句型與文法放大鏡

① 在 Chapter 1 1-4 的文法應用解析、深入應用補一補裡，我們學過不定詞 To V／動名詞 Ving 做主詞。如果主詞不定詞／動名詞太長，聽眾很久才會聽到動詞（頭重腳輕），此時可以將不定詞移到動詞（片語）後，把 it 放在原主詞的位置，當虛主詞（又稱「假主詞」，對照不定詞／動名詞是真的主詞）。句型如下：

It	is	Adj / N	+ To –V / V ing	for N
假主詞			真主詞	對……而言

例 1 To classify movies for children and teenagers is necessary.（對兒童和青少年而言，電影分級制度是必要的。）

提點 此例不定詞所帶的片語共有 7 個字，比較動詞只有一個字（is），形容詞只有一個字，明顯頭重腳輕，所以必須用虛（假）主詞構句比較合適：It is necessary to classify movies for children and teenagers.

例 2 It is the government's duty to require computer games and some publications to have a classification clearly displayed.（要求電腦遊戲和一些出版物必須要有明確的展示分級是政府的責任。）

提點 此例當中不定詞片語（劃線部分）更長了，所以絕對要用虛主詞構句，是名詞（the government's duty）作補語的示範。

例 3 It is not recommended viewing or playing by children under 15 without guidance from parents or guardians.（15 歲以下的兒童在沒有家長或監護人的指導之下就觀看或是播放是不被推薦的。）

提點 此例當中動名詞片語（劃線部分）長了，所以要用虛主詞構句。

 文法和口說應用大結合

以上文法和句型可以運用到 IBT、NEW TOEIC 及 IELTS 考試上面，以下列的題目舉例 Track 06

What do you think of the classification of a movie? Do you think it is necessary? Explain why.

你對電影分級制度的想法如何？你認為有其必要性嗎？請解釋原因。

 高分範文

It is necessary to classify movies especially for children and teenagers. Movies may contain some language or scenes which are not suitable for children and teenagers. For example, movies may contain content which confuses or upsets children. In such cases, children may need the guidance of their parents or guardians.

電影分級制度是必要的特別是對兒童和青少年而言。電影可能包含一些不適合兒童和青少年觀看的語言或是場景。如，電影可能會包含一些混亂和令人孩童生氣的內容。在這些情況之下，兒童可能需要他們家長或是監護人的指導。

Another example is that movies may include violence and nudity of moderate impact or worse; therefore they are not recommended for children under 15 years. Sex scenes and drug use which have a strong impact on children and teenagers should particularly be avoided. Putting it all together, the classification of a movie is very necessary. With the classification of symbols and words which can be seen on posters, advertisements or any advertising materials for films, parents and guardians can use them to determine which films are the most suitable for their children to see.

另一個例子是，電影可能包含中等或更糟的影響程度的暴力和裸體；因此他們不推薦給兒童 15 歲以下的兒童。性愛場景和濫用毒品可能有對孩童和青少年會有很強的影響，應該特別避免。綜合起來，電影分級制度是非常必要的。在海報廣告或是任何廣告有了分級的符號和文字，家長和監護人就可以用這些來為孩子決定哪些是最合適觀看的電影。

關鍵單字解密

1. scene *n.* 場景	2. suitable *adj.* 合適的
3. confuse *v.* 混亂	4. upset *v.* 生氣
5. guardian *n.* 監護人	6. impact *n.* 影響
7. be avoided *ph.* 被避免	

文法應用解析、深入應用補一補

❶ In such cases, children may need the guidance by their parents or guardians.

解析

In such a case, 意思是在那樣的情形下，所以你必須先說是那樣的情形。此例是 "Movies may contain content which confuses or upsets children." 的情形。

其它應用 1

Movies may contain content which have a negative impact on children. In such cases, there should be classification information stated on classified products so that parents can make choices for their children.（電影可能包含對兒童有負面影響的內容。在這樣的情況之下，

產品上應該要有分級資訊，家長才可以為他們的孩子做選擇。）

其它應用 2

A film is classified as 'M' due to its moderate impact. In such a case, it's not recommended for children under 15 years.（電影被分類為 M 級是因為它的中度影響。這個情況之下，不推薦給 15 歲以下的兒童觀看。）

❷ Putting it all together, the classification of a movie is very necessary.

解析

'Putting it all together'（中文：「綜合起來」），可以解釋為表示條件的獨立分詞構句，如果把它還原成一般正常的子句時，寫法是："If we put it all together'..." 因為獨立分詞構句中的主詞如果是 we, you 等泛稱的主詞的時候，是可以省略的。

其它應用

Putting it all together, we should be in favor of the classification of a movie and computer games.（綜合起來，我們應該贊成對電影和電腦遊戲的分級。）

2-1 私立學校和公立學校之利弊

｜應用句型｜
It is well-known that ...／眾所皆知……

｜搭配口說主題｜
私立學校和公立學校之利弊

重點文法搶先看

① 被動語態

② It's well-known that...（眾所皆知的……）

重要句型與文法放大鏡

① **被動語態**：被動語態的目的是<u>**強調動詞的接受者**</u>，也就是受詞，或者是<u>**不知動作者**</u>（也就是主詞）時用被動語態，除此之外，應盡量少使用被動語態。方法是主詞與受詞位置對調，解析如下：

句型：

★ **主動**：主詞 A＋一般動詞＋受詞 B

★ **被動**：主詞 B＋be＋Vpp.＋（介系詞＋受詞 A）

提點（Vpp. 指過去分詞）（通常為：by~）。主詞受詞位置對調時，除了本身需做變化（例：I→by me；

she→by her），動詞的語態也跟著由主動（一般動詞）→被動（be 動詞＋Vpp.過去分詞）例：

★ **主動**：I criticized him.我批評他。

★ **被動**：He was criticized by me.他被我批評。

② **本單元的基本句型介紹的是**：It's well-known that... .（眾所周知的），其中 known 是 know 的過去分詞（Vpp.）。很多人知道，所以是誰知道（主詞是誰），並不重要，重點是那件事實。這句話同學想想看怎麼說：

例句 在美國很多有名的成功的人士是畢業於名聞遐邇的昂貴的私立學校，這是眾所周知的事情。

提點 It's well-known that in the US, a number of famous successful people graduated from reputable expensive private schools.

文法和口說應用大結合

以上文法和句型可以運用到 IBT、NEW TOEIC 及 IELTS 考試上面，以下列的題目舉例 Track 07

People want the best education for themselves or their children. There is much debate about private schools and public/state schools. What are the advantages and disadvantages of these two types of schools?

人們都想自己或自己的孩子受最好的教育。關於私立學校和公立學校有許多爭論。這兩類學校的優勢和劣勢是什麼？

高分範文

Well, let me start with private schools. Firstly, I will talk about class sizes. They tend to be smaller at private schools, and therefore, private schools usually have better teacher-student ratios. The benefits coming from those schools are that pupils gain much greater attention from teachers. As a result, students' particular

好的，讓我先從私立學校開始。首先，我會談班級大小。私立學校的傾向是比較小的班級。因此，私立學校通常有較好的師生比。這些學校的好處就是中小學生可以得到老師更多的注意力。結果，學生在學業上有特別的需要

academic needs and weaknesses are easier to be noticed by teachers. On the other hand, it is well-known that their tuition fees are hugely expensive, which is the major drawback.

或是弱點都可以比較容易被老師注意到。在另一方面，眾所周知的是他們巨量昂貴的學費，這就是最大的缺點。

In contrast, public schools are more affordable, and generally speaking, public school teachers are more highly qualified than private school teachers. If public schools can acquire enough funding from the government, they can have more access to resources and technology than private schools which cannot acquire sufficient funding. The disadvantages come from their larger class sizes. Pupils get less attention from teachers, and this results in disappointment by parents. So my conclusion is, I

對照之下，公立學校比較付得起，而且一般而言，公立學校老師比私立學校老師合格很多。如果公立學校可以從政府那得到足夠的經費，他們可以有更多的機會得到比無法獲得足夠經費的私立學校更多資源和科技。而缺點是他們較多的班級人數。中小學生會獲得老師較少的注意力，這導致了家長的不滿意。總結是，有天份和聰明的孩子在任何學校都可以蓬

believe a gifted and intelligent child can thrive and succeed in any school, while a less intelligent child may benefit from the extra academic attention at private school. Parents and students should gather sufficient information about the school in order to make an informed choice.

勃發展，而較不聰明的孩子可以在私立學校，因為學業上受到特別的重視而獲益。我相信父母和學生應該收集關於學校足夠的資訊，以作出充份的選擇。

關鍵單字解密

1. teacher-student ratio *n.* 師生比	2. As a result *ph.* 結果
3. academic *adj.* 學業上的、學術的	4. drawback *n.* 缺點

文法應用解析、深入應用補一補

❶ ... pupils can gain much greater attention from teachers. As a result, students' particular academic needs and weaknesses are easier to be noticed by teachers.

解析

"As a result, …"（結果/因此，…）是連接因果的重要句型，前句是因，句型：**因句… As a result, 果句**。

其它應用

Students acquire promptly support from their teachers. As a result, they make progress on their academic performance.（他們獲得老師的立即支持。因此，他們在學業表現上有進步。）

❷ ... a gifted and intelligent child can thrive and succeed in any school, while a less intelligent child may benefit from the extra academic attention at private school.

解析

while 是用來對照在比較的兩者之間的不同之處，中文可以翻作「而」，也可以翻成這兩個字原本的意思－「當」（還是在比較）。句型：**A 子句，while B 子句**.

其它應用

Small class sizes can improve discipline, while it's harder for teachers to maintain control of a larger group.（小規模的班級可以改善紀律，而較大的班級使老師在控管上較困難。）**提點** 前後兩個子句對調也可以，把 while 放在句首：**While A 子句，B 子句**.

2-2 描述現行教育入學體制（甄選和考試）

｜應用句型｜
How ...!／（某人／某事）如此……的啊！

｜搭配口說主題｜
描述現行教育入學體制

重點文法搶先看

① How、What 為首的感嘆句

重要句型與文法放大鏡

① 感嘆句用來表示對人事或物讚美、驚訝、喜悅等感嘆情緒，通常以 How 或 What 為首，其中 what 後接名詞，how 後接形容詞或副詞，例如：

例 1 What a (difficult) test！或 What a (difficult) test it was！多麼難的考試呀！或：

例 2 How difficult! 或 How difficult the test was! 多麼難的考試呀！

注意

1. 因為是表示感嘆，句尾當然是用驚嘆號！不是用問號。
2. what 後接名詞，但是在名詞之前可以加形容詞，重點是：一定要接名詞！

基本句型如下

1. **What＋（a/an）＋（形容詞）＋名詞！** 句中的名詞是不可數或是複數時，則 a/an 便需去掉。

2. **How＋形容詞／副詞！** 這種句型後面可以再加主詞和動詞，句型如下：

★ **What＋(a/an)＋（形容詞）＋名詞＋主詞＋動詞！**（如上例 1）

★ **How＋形容詞／副詞＋主詞＋動詞**！（如上例 2）

注意

1. 句中的名詞是與後面主詞同一個/位，由主詞決定名詞單複數，動詞的單複數跟著主詞決定。2. 兩種句型可互換，互換時冠詞使用可能不一樣，如上 2 例（What a difficult test! 或 How difficult the test was!）。3. 前面用名詞，後面的主詞就用代名詞。

② **口試時，當你敘述下列的文字時……**

There were fewer universities 20 years ago. The entrance examinations only took place once a year. The students were under a lot of pressure from these highly competitive exams.（20 年前，大學比較少。入學考試一年只考一次。學生們在這個高度競爭的考試之下，承受相很大的壓力。）**你可以接著說** How demanding those exams are! **或**：What demanding exams those are! **這些考試要求真高啊**！

文法和口說應用大結合

以上文法和句型可以運用到 IBT、NEW TOEIC 及 IELTS 考試上面，以下列的題目舉例 Track 08

How can students go to university? Describe pathways for a student to go to university in your country.
學生如何能進入大學？請描述在你國家進入大學的管道。
也可以應用到這個題目："Describe a typical day for a student in your country". 請描述在你國家的學生典型的一天。

高分範文

In the past, there used to be only one pathway to university, which was to pass the National University Entrance Exams. Now it has become an alternative. This is a united exam, which means the entrance criteria set by any university are based on the same exams. You can enter any university of your desire as long as your scores meet their

在過去只有一個進入大學的方式，就是通過國家大學入學考試。現在它已經變成一種選擇方式。這是一個聯合的考試，表示任何學校都是基於同樣的考試來設定的入學標準。你可以進入你想要唸的大學，只要你的分數達到他們的要求。20 年以

requirements. Twenty years ago, there were fewer universities than there are now. Therefore, it was very demanding to go to any university. Students needed to study very hard. They went to cram schools at nights and slept less than eight hours a day. You can only imagine how excited the students and their parents were when the students could go to their ideal university!

前大學比現在少。因此要進任何大學都有嚴格要求的。學生需要非常努力讀書，在晚上上補習班，並且一天睡眠少於 8 個小時。你只能想像當學生能夠進入他們理想的大學，這些學生和他們的家長會有多麼的興奮！

Meanwhile, this pathway concerned parents greatly because the children were under too much pressure from the annual highly competitive entrance examinations. To address parents' concerns, Taiwan has been through several educational reforms. The main change is to add another pathway

同時，令家長最很擔心的是，孩子們因為這每年一次的高度競爭的入學考試，招承受很大的壓力。為回應家長們的擔心台灣已經經歷了幾次的教育改革。主要的變化是增加人另外一個途徑入學。那就是，學術表現不再是唯

to school. That is, academic performance is not the only criteria to go to a good university; students can apply to a school as long as they have at least one outstanding talent in any area, such as music or football.

一進入好大學的準則。只要學生有至少一項在任何領域，像是音樂或是足球傑出的天份，他們就可以申請學校。

關鍵單字解密

1. entrance exams *n.ph.* 入學考試	2. alternative *n.* 替代；選擇
3. criteria *n.* 條件標準	4. requirement *n.* 要求
5. demanding *adj.* 要求嚴格	6. concern *v.* 擔心；關心
7. competitive *adj.* 有競爭性的	8. educational reform *n.* 教育改革、教改

文法應用解析、深入應用補一補

❶ You can enter any university of your desire as long as your scores meet their requirements.

解析

“as long as”（只要），是表條件的附屬連接詞，句型是：**主要子句 as long as＋副詞子句.**，或是兩個子句對調：**As long as＋副詞子句，主要子句.**

注意：主要子句若是未來式，副詞子句要用現在式，而不是用未來式。

其它應用

You can enter any university you want, as long as you work hard enough.（你可以進你想要上的大學，只要你夠用功。）

❷ What concerned parents most was that the children were under too much pressure from the once-a-year highly competitive entrance examinations.

解析

What concerns/concerned ... most is/was (that)... . What 是 the thing which＋V＋受詞的**關係代名詞子句**，將於 Chapter 6 6-4 介紹。Most 是最多最大的意思，這裡沒有比較的意思，所以不用加冠詞 the。

其它應用

What concerned parents most was their children's health.（家長最擔心的是他們孩子的健康。）

2-3 升學考試之公平性批判

｜應用句型｜
If... , ...can...／
如果……，……就能……

｜搭配口說主題｜
升學考試之公平性批判

重點文法搶先看

① Type 0 條件句

② Type 1 條件句

重要句型與文法放大鏡

① 我們常說如果怎樣的話，我就怎樣，或是假如怎樣就好了，但這些轉化成英文就沒有那麼簡單了，它牽涉到假設語氣，必須用條件句。條件句可以標籤為 4 種條件句（type 0, 1, 2, 3），本單元先介紹前兩種條件句，即：Type 0 條件句 and Type 1 條件句。Type 0 條件句（零條件句）會發生的事，可以使用 can, will, may, might, could 等助動詞在條件句，顯示確定。用途還包含自然法則。

例 If your scores from the National University Entrance Exams meet the threshold requirement of the school, you can enter that school.（如果你大學聯考的成績有達到學校要求的門檻，你就可以進入那所學校。）提點 此例是確定的情形。

② Type 1 條件句

我們可以使用 will, may, might, could **等助動詞在條件句，顯示**可能**、但是**不確定**。用途還包含**：給**建議、協議、威脅和警告。**

那麼以下這一句是屬於 Type 0 或 Type 1 條件句？

If you work hard enough, you can acquire high scores in the exams.（如果你夠用功的話，你會在考試當中得到高分。）

提點 這是 Type 1。這是顯示可能、但是不確定的假設語氣。有努力未必有收穫呀！

以下的例子都是顯示可能、但是不確定的假設語氣：

★ If they meet the school's requirements, they can be offered an interview.（如果你達到學校的要求，你就可以參加面試。）

★ If they know some important person on the committee board, they may be favored.（如果他們有認識委員會當中的重要人物，可能會特別有優勢。）

文法和口說應用大結合

以上文法和句型可以運用到 IBT、NEW TOEIC 及 IELTS 考試上面，以下列的題目舉例 Track 09

What are the common pathways for students to go to university in your country? Comment on those pathways. Do you think students have a fair opportunity to go to university?

在你的國家有哪些進入大學的管道？請評論這些管道。你認為學生有公平的進大學的機會嗎？

高分範文

There are two common pathways for students to go to university. One is through the National University Entrance Exams, which have existed for decades. Public universities require higher scores than private ones, because they are smaller in number, have better quality teachers and much cheaper

有兩種常見的入大學方式。其一是經由大學聯考，它已經存在了數十年了。公立學校要求比私立學校較高的分數，因為他們的數量上比較少、師資更好，學費也比要便宜。學生為了要達到他們所要求的分數必須在準備上花很

tuition. It took students lots of hard work on preparation in order to meet the required scores. To make it worse, the exams only took place once a year. Students who aimed for public school were under huge pressure. Demanding though, the exams are undoubtedly fair . Every student takes the same exams at the same time; their names are not revealed on the test sheet. Nobody can take any privilege.

大的功夫。更糟糕的是，這個考試一年只考一次。目標在公立學校的學生面臨很大的壓力。雖然要求嚴苛，但是這個考試的公平性是無庸置疑的。每位學生都在同一時間參加同一個考試。他們的名字不會顯示在考試卷上。沒有任何人可以取得任何特權。

However, more than ten years ago, the Ministry of Education responded to parents' appeals and began to introduce another pathway, that is, admission by application. Students apply for a university with the records of both their school academic and non-

然而，10 年多以前，教育部回應家長的請求，並開始引進另外一個管道，也就是申請入學。學生以學術和非學術的表現的記錄來申請大學。如果他們達到學校的要求，他們就會被提供面試的機會。有

academic performance. If they meet the school's requirements, they can be offered an interview. There could be several chances to allow personal favors toward some students. To conclude, in terms of fairness, I prefer the traditional Entrance Exams to admission by application.

可能會存在對一些學生有利的機會。結論是，就公平性而言，和申請入學比較，我偏好傳統的入學考試。

關鍵單字解密

1. reveal *v.* 呈現、揭露	2. privilege *n.* 特權
3. appeal *v.* 請求、上訴	4. admission by application *n.ph.* 申請入學
5. non-academic performance *n.ph.* 非學業表現	

文法應用解析、深入應用補一補

❶ To make it worse, the exams only took place once a year.

解析

此例句是不定詞片語作副詞用修飾整個句子，牽涉到 make

的用法，即：**make＋受詞＋形容詞比較（than…）**（使…變得更…）"To make it worse"（讓它變得更糟糕），通俗的中文是「更糟的是」。

其它應用

To make it worse, there were only a few public universities.（更糟的是，那時只有幾所公立大學。）

❷ In terms of fairness, I prefer the traditional Entrance Exams to admission by application.

解析

其中的 "term" 是「條件、條款」的意思；"In terms of" 就是「以／就…而言」，「以…來看（一件事／物）」。

其它應用 1

In terms of tuition fees, private universities are far more expensive than public ones.（就學費而言，私立大學比公立大學要貴很多。）

其它應用 2

In terms of teaching quality, I would say it depends on individual schools and individual teachers.（以教學品質而言，我會說這因學校和老師而異。）

2-4 對教育改革的建議、升學考試之批判

｜應用句型｜
If... could/would...／如果……，……就將……

｜搭配口說主題｜
對教育改革的建議、升學考試之批判

重點文法搶先看

① 與現在事實相反，或稱 Type 2；條件句用過去式

② 與過去事實相反，或稱 Type 3；條件句用過去完成式

重要句型與文法放大鏡

假設語氣依純粹條件，或有可能發生的，或與事實相反的情形可區分為三：

1. 現在與未來皆有可能發生，條件句（if 子句）用現在式之 Type 0, 1，在 2-3 有說明。
2. 與現在事實相反，或稱 Type 2；條件句用過去式；
3. 與過去事實相反，或稱 Type 3；條件句用過去完成式

以下將針對第 2、3 點作分析：

① **與現在事實相反，Type 2 條件句**

If+S+過去式 V , S+would/ could/ might... .+V

提點 **注意**前後的 S 未必代表相同的人事物。例 If it were not for admission by application as an alternative, Donna could not study in her university as an English major. The English department in her university does not value much math scores, which is Donna's weakness.（如果沒有申請入學的選擇的話，Donna 不可能在她的大學主修英文。她的大學的英語系並不看重數學分數，那正好是 Donna 的弱點。）

解析 這是與現在事實相反；Donna 現在有申請入學，她也在大學主修英文。

② **與過去事實相反，Type3 條件句**

If+S+had +Vpp, S+would/could / might... have+Vpp.

例 If the exams had taken place twice a year, the students, in the past, would have been under less pressure.（如果考試一年考兩次，過去的學生壓力就少很多。）

提點 這句是與過去事實相反；考試一年沒有考兩次，之前的學生壓力也沒有減少。

文法和口說應用大結合

以上文法和句型可以運用到 IBT、NEW TOEIC 及 IELTS 考試上面，以下列的題目舉例 Track 10

Talk about the educational systems in your country. What suggestions would you make for education in your country?
談你國家的教育系統。你會對你國家的教育做哪些建議呢？

高分範文

Although there is a plan to extend compulsory education to 12 years, at present, students receive nine years of school education until the age of 15. After graduation, these young people have to face choices. Our society values education since a long time ago; therefore, most students take the competitive entrance examinations for senior high school, while fewer go to vocational school. Another three years later, they can decide

雖然有擴展義務教育到 12 年的計劃；目前，學生接受 9 年的學校教育，直到 15 歲。畢業後，這些年輕人就必須面對選擇。由於我們的社會從很久以前就重視教育，因而大部分的學生參加競爭很激烈的高中入學考試，而很少數的學生進職業學校。在 3 年後，他們可以選擇是否要繼續進大學。對這兩階段的學校

whether to go further to university. For both levels of schools, there are two common pathways to do it: taking the traditional national school entrance exams or applying for admission.

來說，通常有兩種管道入學：參加傳統國家入學考試或是申請入學。

Applying for admission is a new product from the Ministry of Education, after referred to some western countries' prevailing pathways. They thought students could have been under less pressure with this new pathway. On the contrary, such educational reform is under severe criticism. For one thing, it does not help reduce the students' burden. For another, this form can be easier manipulated by people who have power.

申請入學是教育部考慮一些西方國家盛行的入學管道之後的新產物。他們認為學生可以在這一個新的管道之下，壓力可以減少。相反的是，如此的教育改革遭受嚴重批評。一方面它並沒有幫助減輕學生的負擔。另一方面，這一個形式容易被有權力的人所操縱。

To take these drawbacks into consideration, I strongly propose

考慮了這些缺點，我提議傳統的入學考試

traditional entrance exams remain and be held twice a year.	應該維持，並且一年舉辦兩次。

▸▸ 關鍵單字解密

1. prevailing *adj.* 盛行的

2. severe criticism *v.* 嚴重批評

文法應用解析、深入應用補一補

❶ For one thing, it does not help reduce the students' burden. For another, this form can be easier manipulated by people who have power.

解析

For one thing, ... For another…（一方面是…，另一方面是…），常用在列舉事實、原因等。

其它應用

The new alternative doesn't help. For one thing, it doesn't help to reach the goal of reducing students' needs for cram schools. For another, some parents and students believe that every score from school counts in applying to universities. As a result, those students burn midnight oil everyday.（這個新的替代方法並沒有幫助。一

方面，它對達成減少學生上補習班需要的目標並沒有幫助。另一方面，一些家長和學生相信在校的每一次成績都會算入申請大學。結果，這些學生每晚都熬夜挑燈夜戰。）

❷ To take these drawbacks into consideration, I strongly propose traditional entrance exams remain and be held twice a year.

解析

現在介紹一組特殊單字的特殊用法：建議、命令、請求、堅持的句型：

★ **S+V+(that)+S+(should)+V/be**（！易錯）

★ 以上 V 的位置可置放以下單字，另外除了 suggest, propose, demand, insist 之外，都可以用 S+V+O+to-V **的句型**，如：I advise you to read my book.（我建議你閱讀我的書。）

建議	命令	請求	堅持
propose 提議 suggest 建議 advise 忠告 recommend 推薦 urge主張	commend demand	request	insist

其它應用

I urge there should be some mechanism to prevent anyone from being treated unfairly.（我主張應該有一個機制，來防範任何人受到不公平的對待。）

2-5 學生自主學習的必要性

應用句型		搭配口說主題
I wish... / I hope... ／ 我希望……		學生自主學習的必要性

重點文法搶先看

① wish、if only 與假設語氣的連用

② 與現在事實相反的句型

③ 與過去事實相反的句型

重要句型與文法放大鏡

假設語氣除了與 If 子句、otherwise 連用，也常與 wish, if only, 連用：wish（但願）假設語氣表示希望，但是不可能實現的，例如 40 歲的女人永遠不會變為 20 歲的女孩。與 if only（要是怎樣就好了），可以互換。

① **與現在事實相反時的句型：**

S wish＋S 過去式 V.、**If only＋S 過去式 V.**

例 1 I wish my class had more open discussions. 以及 If only my class had more open discussions.（但願我的

課程能夠有更多開放式的討論。）

例 2 I wish/ If only our learners had more autonomy in deciding their own learning. 但願我們的學習者，在決定他們自己的學習方面，能夠有更多的自主權。

② **與過去事實相反時的句型：**

S wish＋S **would/could/might have＋Vpp or had＋Vpp**

If only＋S **would/could/might have＋Vpp or had＋Vpp**

例 I wish/If only I could have known cooperative learning earlier. It is a very effective way of learning. Students work cooperatively in small groups; each group member shares responsibility for the outcome.（但願我當時能夠早些了解合作學習。它是一個非常有效率的學習方式。學生以小組合作；每一小組的成員都對結果有責任。

再來看看 hope **的用法**：I wish I had received the education which gives students more autonomy. However, I hope this cooperative learning will happen in the near future.（但願之前我所接受的教育是給學生更多的自主權的。然而，我希望在不久的將來，合作學習能夠發生。） 提點 hope 是希望不是不可能實現的某事發生時用，後面接 that 子句，that 可省略。**這句是現在希望**所以**子句後用現在式助動詞－**will。

文法應用解析、深入應用補一補

以上文法和句型可以運用到 IBT、NEW TOEIC 及 IELTS 考試上面，以下列的題目舉例 Track 11

Talk about your experience at school. Describe what your class is or was like, and things you think can be or could have been improved.

請談談你的學校經驗。請描述你現在或過去的課程是什麼樣子的，還有你認為可以改善的部份。

高分範文

Speaking from my own experience, I wish I had received an education that gives students more autonomy, share opinions about or even designing what to learn, or the curriculum. I urge that students should take more active roles in learning, instead of being passive learners.

就我自己的經驗而言，我希望我之前接受的教育是能給學生更多自主權的，分享意見，甚至設計學習內容或是課綱。我主張學生在學習上應該採取更主動的角色，而不是只當被動的學習者。

The first reason that comes

我能想到的第一個

to my mind is this helps them develop critical thinking and creativity. Taiwanese students have been criticized for rote learning, that is, to memorize before they understand. In the long run, they don't enjoy learning on their own from reading books. They won't enjoy exploring knowledge by themselves.

理由是，這樣能夠幫助他們發展批判性思考和創造力。台灣的學生一直被批被批評死背學習，那就是，在了解之前先背起來。長期而言，他們如果不能享受靠自己讀書學習的樂趣，他們就不會喜愛自己探索知識。

Teachers cannot make learning happen but can only influence its focus, speed and direction. According to some scholars, knowledge is generated by learners participating in classroom activities. This is because without their participation, there would be nothing to think about and no way of understanding what is read or observed.

老師們不能讓學習發生，但是能夠影響學習的焦點、速度和方向。根據一些學者，知識是由學習者參與教室活動所產生的。這是因為沒有參與，就沒有思考，也就沒有了解他們所讀的或是觀察到的。

關鍵單字解密

1. autonomy *n.* 自主權	2. curriculum *n.* 課綱
3. passive *adj.* 被動的	4. critical *adj.* 批判的
5. creativity *n.* 創造力	6. rote learning *n.* 死背學習

文法應用解析、深入應用補一補

❶ I urge that students should take more active roles in learning, instead of being passive learners.

解析

instead of 是介係詞片語，意思是「而不是……」後方需接名詞或動名詞（V-ing）。

其它應用 1

Instead of using rote learning as the only way of learning, students need to understand first and discuss with peers. They gain knowledge through finding, synthesizing, analysing and interpreting information.（不以死背學習法為唯一的學習方式，學生們應該先了解，然後和同儕討論。他們經由發現、合成、分析和解讀信息來獲得知識。）

其它應用 2

Instead of transmitting the content on the textbooks, teachers should provide opportunities for students to explore knowledge by themselves.（教師應該提供給學生自己探索知識的機會，而不是只傳授教科書上的內容。）

❷ According to some scholars, knowledge is generated by learners participating in classroom activities.

解析

"According to" 是介系詞片語，意思是「根據……」，後方需接名詞或動名詞（V-ing）。

其它應用 1

According to some statistics, cooperative learning contributes to learning more effectively than working individually.（根據一些統計數字，合作學習對學習的幫助比獨自學習更有效。）

其它應用 2

According to some sources, students learn more effectively when they know how to manage their own learning.（根據一些來源，當學生知道怎麼去管理他們自己的學習時，他們會學得更有效率。）

2-6 男女分校或是合校

｜應用句型｜
It is... who/that...／
正是……（某人／某事）……

｜搭配口說主題｜
男女分校或是合校

重點文法搶先看

① 可強調語氣的句型、分裂句句型

重要句型與文法放大鏡

強調句或強調結構的使用是為了加強某個字詞、片語或者句子的語氣。通常採用分裂句－ "It is...that" 的句型，或是採用詞序變換的方式。把強調的部分往前移，表示「就是」、「正是」等語詞來強調語氣。

① 可強調語氣的句型、分裂句句型：

It is/was **強調的部分**＋**關係詞代名詞（通常用 that 可省略）**（＋S）＋V

提點 可用來加強句中的某一要素：主詞、受詞、副詞、副詞片語或子句皆可，句子以 It（形式主詞）開頭之後接 be（is/

was），把要強調的字或片語放在 be 動詞之後。

★ 強調主詞-人時，用主格關係代名詞 who（可用 that）

★ 強調受詞-人時，用受格關係代名詞 whom（可用 that）

★ 強調主詞、受詞-物時，用受格關係代名詞 which（可用 that）

★ 強調地方副詞時，用關係副詞 where（可用 that）

★ 強調時間副詞時，用關係副詞 when（可用 that）

例 1 It is parents who/that often choose schools for their children.（正是家長為他們的孩子選擇學校。）

提點 強調主詞－人－是 parents，不是其他人或其他因素。

例 2 It is student's and parents' preferences which/that determine the choice.（正是學生和家長的偏好是這個選擇的決定因素。）

提點 強調主詞-物--student's and parents' preferences

例 3 It is dividing boys and girls into separate classrooms which/that actually delays the development of their interpersonal communication skills.（正是將男生和女生分開教室上課，確實延遲了他們人際溝通技巧的發展。）

提點 強調主詞－物－ dividing boys and girls into separate classrooms

文法和口說應用大結合

以上文法和句型可以運用到 IBT、NEW TOEIC 及 IELTS 考試上面，以下列的題目舉例 Track 12

There has been much debate as to whether single-sex schools provide a better education than their co-ed counterparts, or vice versa. What are the pros and cons of both types of schools? 對於男女合校或是分校何種是較好的教育一直是有很多的爭論。這兩種學校的優點跟缺點各是如何是什麼呢？

高分範文

Surely both types of schools have their pros and cons. Let me start with single sex schools. The main reason for people to propose single sex schools is to avoid distraction from the other sex, so students can concentrate on study. Another benefit of single sex schools would be students may feel more comfortable in schools without the presence of other sex.

的確兩種學校都各有他們的優缺點。讓我由男女分校開始。對很多人來說，提倡男女分校的主要原因是可以避免對異性分心，所以學生能專心於學習。另一個分校的好處是學生會在學校，沒有異性同學在場時，會覺得比較自在。

On the other hand, the separation also deprives students the opportunity to learn to understand the other sex. It affects their development of interpersonal communication skills, which is so important in the real world.

然而在另一方面，這個分離也剝奪了學生學習了解異性的機會。這影響到了他們人際溝通的技巧的發展，這技巧在現實社會是很重要的。

In terms of the benefit of co-ed classrooms, girls can learn to understand the thoughts and feelings of boys, and vice versa. On the other hand, girls, especially, may pay too much attention on their physical appearance. They may take a lot of time to put on make-up and do their hair before going to school. Another drawback is that students may be less comfortable participating in class discussions and activities due to the presence of the other sex.

就男女合校的利益而言，女孩子可以了解男孩子的想法和感覺，反之亦然。在另一方面，特別是女孩子可能會太注意到她們的外表。她們可能會在上學前花很多時間在化妝和髮型上面。另一個缺點是學生可能在參與班級討論和活動，因為異性的在場，而比較不自在。

關鍵單字解密

1. deprive *v.* 剝奪	2. interpersonal communication *n.* 人際溝通
3. vice versa 反之亦然	4. physical appearance *n.* 外表

文法應用解析、深入應用補一補

❶ Another benefit of **single sex schools** would be **students may feel more comfortable at schools without their co-ed counterparts' presence.**

解析

"Another benefit of... . would be... ."這個句型常用來說明還有的好處。因為這是想法、推論，所以不用"will"，用"would"，同學要注意。

其它應用

Another benefit of co-ed would be students can be exposed to the thoughts, feelings and the perspectives of more than just the single sex counterparts.（合校教育的另外一個好處就是，學生可以接觸在非單一性別同學的想法、感覺和觀點。）

❷ Students may be less comfortable participating in class discussions and activities due to the presence of the other sex.

解析

介系詞片語——“due to”，相當於 because of，後面接名詞或動名詞。

其它應用

Due to focusing on their physical appearance to look attractive to other students, both male and female students in co-ed settings may spend more time on physical appearance than study.（因為注重他們的外表以吸引其他的學生，在男女合校的男生和女生都可能花很多時間在外表上，而不是學習上。）

3-1 談家鄉的環境／變遷

｜應用句型｜
both A and B.／
A 和 B 都……

｜搭配口說主題｜
談家鄉的環境／變遷

重點文法搶先看

① 主要子句，and/but/or 對等子句

② 對等連接詞群組和 “and” 的使用

重要句型與文法放大鏡

連接詞是用來連接單字、片語、子句，依其連接成份不同分為兩類：對等連接詞和附（從）屬連接詞。本單元的焦點是對等連接詞。對等連接詞連接的句子可獨立存在，它們地位相等，所以稱為對等子句。對等連接詞有 and, but, or 等。

① and, but, or 可連接子句

句型：**主要子句，and/but/or 對等子句**

例 Originally, it was only Taiwanese aboriginals who lived in this beautiful territory, **and** later some immigrants from mainland China came **and** claimed that they were the owners of this land.（起初，只有台灣的原住民居住在這個美麗的領土，之後一些從中國大陸來的移民，聲稱他們是這片土地的主人。）

② **其中只有 "and" "or" 可連接任何詞性的單字**

例 After 1949, Taiwan experienced economic success; people's income **and** living standards have been significantly improved.（在 1949 年後，台灣經歷了經濟起飛，在所得和生活水準上都隨之有了顯著的提高。）

③ **以下的對等連接詞群組和 "and" 的使用：**

★ **both A and B**（A 和 B 都是）V 複（動詞用複數動詞）

例 Both typhoons and earthquakes hit Taiwan and bring casualties.（颱風和地震兩者都侵襲台灣，並帶來傷亡事故。）

★ **A as well as B**（A 和 B 一樣）Va（動詞與 A 配合）

例 Taiwan as well as Japan is under the risk of earthquakes.（台灣和日本一樣都受地震的威脅。）

文法和口說應用大結合

以上文法和句型可以運用到 IBT、NEW TOEIC 及 IELTS 考試上面，以下列的題目舉例 Track 13

Tell about your hometown/country. Describe what it is like now and any changes from the past. 請談你的家鄉／國家。描述它現在的樣子以及與過去不同的改變。

高分範文

Great! I like to talk about Taiwan, my country, and share this wonderful country with people. First of all, it is an island in East Asia, near Hong Kong. Its shape is like a yam or a whale, depending on which angle you take. It's a small island, but crowded with a population of 23 million!

太棒了！我很喜歡談我的國家——台灣，並且與人分享這個美妙的國家。首先，這是位於東亞的島嶼，靠近香港。它的形狀像是地瓜或是鯨魚，這取決於你用什麼角度來看。它是一個小島，但是很擁擠，擁有 2 千 3 百萬的人口。

Taipei is the capital city. It is one of the most modern and

台北市是首都，它是世界上最現代且最昂

expensive cities to live in in the world. The building, Taipei 101, used to be the highest building in the world; however, it becomes the ninth, according to the data in 2011. When I was a child, the **cost of living** was not as high as it is now. Now I live in Kaohsiung, the second biggest city in Taiwan. It is a marvelous harbour city; it is warm all the year around.

貴的居住城市之一。台北 101 大樓之前是世界上最高的建築物；而根據在 2011 年的資料，現在已經是第九名。當我是孩子的時候，它的生活成本沒有現在這麼高。現在我住在高雄市，台灣的第二大城市。這是一個很奇妙的港口城市；一整年都很暖和

Though the climate is generally pleasant, there are on average three to four typhoons every year. Another significant natural **hazard** is earthquakes. Both typhoons and earthquakes can bring casualties.

雖然天氣一般來說都是很愉悅的，但是台灣一年有三到四個颱風侵襲。另外一個顯著的天然危害是地震。颱風和地震兩者都可能帶來傷亡事故。

What I like best about Taiwan is that living there is very

我最喜歡台灣的部分是它的生活非常方便。有 24 小時的購物

convenient. There are 24 hour shopping malls, movie theaters and bookstores. Besides, the 24 hour convenience stores, such as 7-11, are everywhere and sell almost everything. Also, I would say the most precious treasure of Taiwan is the Taiwanese hospitality. Most Taiwanese are very friendly. I think you would agree with me!

中心，電影院和書店。此外，24 小時的便利商店，像是 7-11，到處都有，幾乎什麼東西都有賣。而且，我會説台灣最珍貴的寶藏，就是台灣人的熱情好客。大部分的台灣人都非常友善。我想你一定會同意我的！

關鍵單字解密

1. cost of living *n.* 生活成本	2. hazard *n.* 危害

文法應用解析、深入應用補一補

❶ Its shape is like a yam or a whale, depending on which angle you take.

解析

“depending on”是分詞構句= 由 “it depends on ⋯.” 簡化而來 “depending on which angle/viewpoint you take” 這一個構句的意思是「⋯。取決於你用什麼角度／觀點來看而定」。

其它應用

Street vendors and sale stands occupy street sides and pavements and billboards are hung everywhere; you can consider them to be either convenient or messy, depending on which viewpoint you take.（街頭小販和販賣攤位佔據了街道兩邊和人行道，以及到處都掛著廣告牌；你可以認為它們是方便的，或是亂七八糟，這取決於你用什麼觀點來看而定。）

❷ The building, Taipei 101, used to be the highest building in the world.

解析

"used to+v" 表示後面這個動作（v），只在過去發生，現在已經停止了，所以 use 用過去式－used，to 後面加原形動詞。

其它應用

There have been significant changes in the landscape of modern cities. For example, I know many areas in Taipei used to be resident areas but have now been transformed into busy commercial areas.（這些現代城市的風貌已經有很顯著的改變。例如，我知道很多台北的地區，之前是住宅區，而現在已經改變成很繁忙的商業區。）

3-2

談全球環境問題

應用句型		搭配口說主題
neither..or...		談全球環境問題
不是 … 就是 …		

重點文法搶先看

① A or B V（A 或 B）（V: 動詞與 B 配合）

② either A or B（不是 A 就是 B）（V: 動詞與 B 配合）

③ neither A nor B（不是 A 也不是 B）（V: 動詞與 B 配合）

重要句型與文法放大鏡

① **A or B V**（A 或 B）（V：動詞與 B 配合）

例 1 Making changes to save the Globe is not easy; there are so many different factors coming into play. People may have the desire to stick to their routines, or **do not** consider that what they do will affect future generations.

（做出改變以救地球並不容易；有太多的不同的因素運作在一起。人們可能想要守著他們的習慣，或是不認為他們所做的會影響未來的世代。）

② **either A or B**（不是 A 就是 B）（V: 動詞與 B 配合）

例 2 Waste disposal hopefully can be reduced by reducing **either** the production **or** the consumption of products which **generate** that waste.

（希望廢棄物可以減少，不是減少生產，就是減少消費會產生廢棄物的產品。）

③ **neither A nor B**（不是 A 也不是 B）（V: 動詞與 B 配合）

例 3 Neither food nor natural resources **are** enough because of the population explosion.

（因為人口爆炸，食物和天然的資源都不足夠。）

文法和口說應用大結合

以上文法和句型可以運用到 IBT、NEW TOEIC 及 IELTS 考試上面，以下列的題目舉例 Track 14

What do you think are the current urgent environmental issues? Describe them and provide solutions.

你認為現在最急迫的環境問題是哪些？請描述它們並提供解決方案。

高分範文

Speaking of current environmental problems, nowadays, people all across the world are facing a wealth of new and challenging environmental problems every day. Some of them are small and only affect a few **ecosystems**, but others have drastic impacts. Undoubtedly, global warming has become top of the list which requires urgent attention. Global warming leads

說起當前的環境問題，在世界各地，人們每天都在面對很多新的和具挑戰的環境問題。一些問題算小，而且只影響到一些生態系統，但是有一些已經有了劇烈的影響。無庸置疑的，全球暖化已經是在名單的首位，需要迫切的注意。全球暖化導致地球表面溫度和海洋溫

to the rise of temperatures of the earth's surface and the oceans. It affects ecosystems significantly.

度的升高。這些造成北極的冰山溶化及海平面升起。這顯著影響到生態系統。

Some people are inclined to hold the view that global warming is caused by human activities, such as burning fossil fuels. The damage caused by such human activities is aggravated by another severe current environmental problem, that is, overpopulation. The population explosion means intensive agriculture is needed to produce food, and this strains the already scarce resources. To meet the high demands of crops, chemical fertilizer, pesticides and insecticides are often used and this further damages the environment.

一些人會傾向認為全球暖化是人類活動所造成的，像是燃燒化石燃料。這些人類活動所造成的損害，因另外一個嚴重的當前環境問題，那就是人口過盛的問題加劇了。人口爆炸意味著必須進行密集的農業以產生食物，這再次擠壓了已經很稀少資源。為了滿足對農作物的高需求，經常使用化學施肥農藥和殺蟲劑造成了對環境進一步的破壞。

In terms of solutions, setting stricter plant emission limit would help to reduce global warming. Implementation of regulation of the birth rate would be a solution for overpopulation. However, there are too many issues accompanying this and these issues need to be considered.

就解決而言，建立更嚴格的廠房排放限制，可以幫忙減少全球暖化。在出生率上進行管制也可以解決人口過盛的問題。然而，需要考慮伴隨而來的太多的問題。

關鍵單字解密

1. a wealth of *n.ph.* 豐富的很多的	2. ecosystem *n.* 生態系統
3. inclined to *ph.* 傾向于	4. aggravate *v.* 加劇

文法應用解析、深入應用補一補

❶ Speaking of current environmental problems, nowadays, people all across the world are facing a wealth of new and challenging environmental problems every day.

解析

"Speaking of ⋯"（說起⋯⋯，談到⋯⋯）用來接過話題，是表示條件的獨立分詞構句，如果把它還原成一般正常的子句時，寫法是："If we speak of …" 因為獨立分詞構句中的主詞如果是 we, you 等泛稱的主詞的時候，是可以省略的。可以用 "Speaking of which, "説起這，可指剛説的事情。

其它應用

Speaking of climate change, it is likely this is the result of human practices, such as emission of greenhouse gases.（説起氣候變遷，它很可能是由人類行為造成的，像是排放溫室氣體。）

❷ Some people **are inclined to** hold the view that global warming is caused by human activities, such as burning fossil fuels.

解析

"be inclined to"（傾向於……，有……的趨勢）."inclined"（傾斜的）；to 是 adv. 到某種狀態的意思；be inclined to ＋v 後面加原形動詞。hold the view 是表示「持這個看法」。

其它應用

Some people **are inclined to** hold the view that noxious emissions from industry plants and motor vehicles are the number one pollutants.（一些人傾向於持有從工廠廠房和機動車輛來的有毒排放物，是第 1 號污染物之看法。）

3-3 談環境保護政策

｜應用句型｜
Unless...／除非

｜搭配口說主題｜
環境保護政策

重點文法搶先看

① 附屬連接詞與 主要子句 **if/unless**… 子句

② Unless 與 as long as

重要句型與文法放大鏡

① **附屬連接詞**：附屬連接詞，包括 because, so, when , after, if ,though ,although, that, who , which, whether, 只接句子，所連接的句子稱附屬子句，不能單獨存在。附屬子句，包括：

★ 名詞子句做名詞用，連接詞有：that, when, where..（見 Chapter 6）

★ 形容詞子句做形容詞用：連接詞有：who, which…,（見 Chapter 6）

★ 副詞子句做副詞用：連接詞有：because, when, if 假

如；unless 除非； in case 以防萬一；as long as 只要

句型公式為 **主要子句 if/unless… 子句** = **If/Unless… 子句**，**主要子句**

以上副詞子句的兩種句型，注意逗號位置表條件的附屬連接詞——if（假如）；unless（除非）；as long as（只要）；in case（以防萬一）

② Unless（除非）

例 Individuals, organizations and governments should collaborate. Environmental protection depends not only on governments' regulations, but also on individuals' and organizations' cooperation. **Unless** these three aspects are addressed together, it will be difficult for environmental protection to become a reality.（個人、機構和政府應該共同合作。環境保護不僅是倚靠政府的管治，也仰賴個人和機構的合作。除非這三方面同時一起解決，否則環保成為事實是很困難的。）

unless **（除非）與** as long as **（只要）有時候可以互換，但是注意它們之間有肯定與否定的差別，同中文的邏輯，** 例 It will **not** be difficult for environmental protection to become a reality, **as long as** these three aspects are addressed together.（只要這三方面同時一起解決，環保成為事實並非難事。）

文法和口說應用大結合

以上文法和句型可以運用到 IBT、NEW TOEIC 及 IELTS 考試上面，以下列的題目舉例 Track 15

Environmental issues have threatened the environment significantly. What do you think individuals, organizations or governments can do to protect the natural environment?
環境的問題已經顯著的威脅到環境。你認為個人、機構或是政府應該做什麼以保護自然環境呢？

高分範文

Indeed, we cannot ignore any more the aggravation of the global environment and it is everybody's responsibility to protect our Earth. For environmental protection to be effective, individuals, organizations and governments should collaborate.

確實，我們不能再忽視地球環境的加劇惡化，保護我們的地球是每一個人的責任。要使環境保護有效，個人、機構和政府都應該合作。

For individuals, it is shocking

就個人可做的來

to know that not everyone agrees that human activity **contributes** directly to environmental issues. In such cases, there should be education to provide facts and ethical concepts. This, hopefully, can create awareness of the various environmental issues.

說，我很驚訝並非每個人都同意人類活動直接對環境問題產生影響。在這個情況之下，應該要有教育來提供事實和道德觀念。希望這可以使人意識到不同的環境問題。

In terms of governments, they should place some regulations on activities that cause environmental **degradation** by industries and set environmental agreements with them. These agreements should at least establish baseline targets, and governments should **monitor** industries on those activities. Furthermore, countries should develop agreements signed by multiple governments to prevent damage or manage

就政府的層面，他們應該設置一些管制在會產生環境惡化的工業活動上，並且和他們設置環境協議。這些協議至少應該要建立基本的目標，政府應該**監督**產業那些活動。更進一步的，更多國家之間應該發展協議，多國國家共同簽署，以避免損害或是管理人類活動對自然資源的影響。這些嘗試已經做到了；其中一個

the impact of human activity on natural resources. Such attempts are made already; one example is the Kyoto Protocol, which focuses on the reduction of greenhouse gas emissions.

例子是「京都議定書」，它的焦點是減少溫室氣體的排放。

In short, environmental protection should be done at all individual, organizational and governmental levels, for the benefit of both the natural environment and humans.

簡而言之，環境保護應該在個人、機構和政府的層面都要做到，同時為了自然環境和人類。

關鍵單字解密

1. collaborate *v.* 合作	2. contribute *v.* 貢獻
3. degradation *n.* 惡化	4. monitor *v.* 監視

文法應用解析、深入應用補一補

❶ Furthermore, more countries should develop agreements signed by multiple governments to prevent damage or manage the impacts of human activity on natural resources.

解析

Further 是 far 的形容詞比較級，有三個含意：在距離上和時間上的更遠；在程度上更大；補充附加之前所說的；furthermore—— 中譯是「更者」、「更進一步」、「還有」、「再者」，類似 in addition、moreover。

其它應用

Moreover, companies should reduce or terminate producing any products which emit pollutants in the process.（再者，公司應該減少或終止產生任何在過程中會排放污染物的產品。）

❷ In short, environmental protection should be done at all individual, organizational and governmental levels.

解析

"In short"（簡而言之），轉折語。最後結尾時強調觀點。

其它應用

In short, both governments' environmental decisions and individuals' environmental values and behaviors determine the effectiveness of environmental protection.（簡而言之，政府的環境決策和個人的環境價值和行為兩者，皆決定環保的有效程度。）

3-4 談交通問題及其影響

|應用句型|
so that 所以能、
in order that 為了／以至於……

|搭配口說主題|
談交通問題及其影響

重點文法搶先看

① in order that 為了

② so that 所以能

重要句型與文法放大鏡

① **主要子句 in order that＋副詞子句＝In order that＋副詞子句，主要子句**

例 1 Some people argue that more parking spaces should be built **in order that** drivers can easily find a place to park.（一些人爭論為了駕駛人能夠容易的找一個位置停車，應該建造更多的停車位。）

提點 "in order that 子句" 有時候可以跟不定詞片語 "in order to＋V" 互換： 例 2 Some people argue that more parking spaces should be built **in order to** allow drivers to park easily.

② **主要子句 so that ＋副詞子句.**

"in order that 子句" 有時候可以跟 "so that＋子句" 互換：

例 1 **Some people argue that more parking spaces should be built** so that **drivers can easily find a place to park.**

提點 so that＋子句. 有時候可以跟不定詞片語 "so as to＋V" 互換：

例 2 **Some people argue that more parking spaces should be built** so as to **allow drivers to park easily.**

請看更多的例子：**例 3** One possible cause of traffic jams is that roads and streets there are too narrow and too few alternative roads to popular destinations. In such cases, the traffic department should understand the situation and plan for changes in order to improve this situation.（造成交通阻塞的一個可能性是道路和街道太窄，或是到熱門目的地替代道路太少。在這種情形之下，交通部門應該要了解這個狀況，並且為改善作計畫。）

文法和口說應用大結合

以上文法和句型可以運用到 IBT、NEW TOEIC 及 IELTS 考試上面，以下列的題目舉例 Track 16

What do you think traffic problems in big cities are? What are your recommendations to those problems?

你認為在大城市的交通問題是什麼？你對這些問題有什麼建議呢？

高分範文

Generally speaking, traffic problems in big cities include too many automobiles, too narrow of roads and streets and too few parking spaces. These are problems that people have to face every day especially in major cities. Too many people drive cars to work, rather than taking public transportation. This may be caused by the fact that cars are so cheap. If this is the

一般來說，在大都市的交通問題是車輛太多、道路和街道太窄，以及停車位太少。這些是在人們每天會面臨的問題，尤其是都會區。太多人開車去上班，而不是搭乘公共交通工具。這個原因可能是汽車太便宜的事實導致的。如果這是事實的話，政府應該要在私人

case, governments should levy higher taxes on private vehicles and raise the price of gasoline in order to discourage the use of private vehicles.

的交通工具上徵收更高的稅，並且提高汽油的成本，以抑制購買和使用私人交通工具。

This may also be caused by the fact that public transportation is not that available. In this case, governments should improve the system. A particular phenomenon in Taiwan is too many motor scooters and motorcycles; they are everywhere, sometimes occupying pavements. It can often be seen that cars fight for space with motorbikes in exclusive motorbike lanes. This behaviour is hazardous not only to drivers but also to pedestrians. To make matters worse, the automobiles generate a great deal of exhaust and this results in

這也可能是因為公共交通工具並不方便取得的事實。在這個情況之下，政府應該改善這個系統。一個在台灣的特別現象是，太多的摩托車和重型機車。他們到處都是，有時候後佔據人行道。通常可以見汽車和摩托車在摩托車專用道上爭道。這種行為不僅危害到駕駛人，也危害到行人。更糟糕的是，車輛產生大量的廢氣，因此導致空氣污染。所以基於這個理由，政府應該管制車輛

air pollution. So, for these reasons, governments should regulate the amount of vehicles.

的數量。

When all these problems happen because of traffic jams, it causes citizens' expensive time costs and finally degrades living conditions. By and large, traffic problems are too serious to neglect.

當這些問題發生在塞車時，導致昂貴的時間成本，並且最終會降低生活狀況。大致說來，交通問題是太嚴重了，以至於無法忽略。

關鍵單字解密

1. levy *v.* 徵收課徵	2. exhaust *n.* 排氣

文法應用解析、深入應用補一補

❶ Too many people drive cars to work, rather than taking public transportation.

解析

rather than 可當「連接詞」，連接形態和詞性對等的字詞，如兩個名詞、兩個動詞（＋ing）或兩個副詞。可以放在主要句子之前或之後。

其它應用

This solution may solve the problem temporarily, rather than radically. 這個解決辦法可能只能暫時的解決問題，而不是根本上的解決。

❷ This may be also caused by the fact that public transportation is not that available.

解析

"may be caused by N"（可能是由什麼 N 造成的），是介系詞後面加名詞或動名詞，也可以加子句－the fact that（什麼的事實）："may be caused by the fact that... "。

其它應用

Difficulty in finding parking spaces may be caused by insufficient parking lots. 停車位難尋可能是因不夠的停車位所造成的。（小補充：停車場英國用 car parks）

3-5 對改善交通問題之建議

| 應用句型 |
Nonetheless,...、in the long run
然而、長遠來說……

| 搭配口說主題 |
對改善交通問題之建議

重點文法搶先看

① 轉折語：就…而言：in terms of... ,

② 轉折語：當談到…時：when it comes to...

③ 轉折語：同時地：meanwhile; in the meantime; at the same time; simultaneously,

重要句型與文法放大鏡

轉折語可提供聽眾和讀者線索，以追尋作者文義。這些語詞包含強調、補充資訊和觀點、表示轉折、順序、前因後果等，注意它們是**連結**語意，而不同連接詞作用是連接兩個子句，如前幾個單元所介紹的。常用的轉折語整理如下。

① 就…而言：in terms of …,

例 In terms of fundamental solutions, I believe only by narrowing the urban-rural gap, the traffic problem can be solved.（就基本的解決方法而言，我相信只有縮小城鄉差距可以解決交通問題。）

② 當談到…時：when it comes to…;as far as 某事／某人 is concerned

例 When it comes to the traffic issue, many people consider congestion as their worst nightmare.（當談到交通問題時，很多人認為塞車是他們最大的夢魘。）

③ 同時地： meanwhile; in the meantime; at the same time; simultaneously,

例 The relevant traffic department should levy more tax on using the roads. Meanwhile, they should provide better quality of public transportation as an alternative.（相關的交通部門應該要徵收更多的使用道路稅。同時他們應該提供更好的公共交通運輸的品質作為替代。）

文法和口說應用大結合

以上文法和句型可以運用到 IBT、NEW TOEIC 及 IELTS 考試上面，以下列的題目舉例 Track 17

What are your recommendations for reducing traffic congestion?

你對解決塞車有什麼建議？

高分範文

Traffic congestion takes its toll on quality of life, driving safety and air quality. It will continue to get worse unless policymakers take steps to intervene. One reason for congestion is an imbalance in the supply of and demand for road space. This problem can be solved by increasing the supply of road space or reducing the demand for peak-hour automotive travel.

開車帶來了生活品質駕駛安全和空氣品質的損害。除非政策決定者能夠採取手段干預，這個問題會持續惡化。塞車的一個原因是道路的供需不平衡。這個問題可以以增加道路空間的供給，以及減少尖峰時候的行駛車輛的需要。

In terms of reducing the demand for travel, one policy can be congestion pricing, which involves charging drivers more for their use of roadways. The strategies include assigning higher tolls for driving during peak hours or collecting higher fees for parking in the most demanding spaces. Strategies also include increasing private cars' import tax and fuel tax in order to reduce the number of the private cars. However, at the same time, it is very important to provide for alternatives for private car owners, that is, either improving the quality and quantity of public transportation, or implementing or increasing bike only lanes.

就減少行駛車輛的需求而言，一個政策可以是塞車成本，也就是涉及向駕駛人索取使用道路費。這些策略包含指定更高的過路費，在駕駛尖峰時刻或是在最需求量最高的停車位上，收更多的停車費。政策也可以包括增加私家車的進口稅和燃料稅，以減少私家家車的數量。然而，非常重要的是，同時間提供的私家車駕駛的替代方案，也就是提高公共運輸的質與量，和安置或增加自行車專用道。

Nonetheless, the

話雖如此，根本的

fundamental strategy for me is narrowing the gap between urban and rural areas. Because of the serious imbalance of development between urban cities and rural areas, many commuters travel to work through tubes and this causes them to be too crowded, such as those in Beijing and London. For this reason, I believe narrowing the urban-rural gap is a radical solution in the long run.

政策對我而言是，縮小都市和鄉村的差距。由於嚴重的發展不平衡，都市和鄉村地區很多通勤者通勤坐地鐵去工作，並造成地鐵太擁擠，像是在北京和倫敦的狀況。基於這個理由，我相信縮小城鄉差距還是在長期根本的辦法。

關鍵單字解密

1. toll *n.* 損失（路橋等的）通行費	2. policymaker *n.* 制定政策者
3. congestion *n.* 阻塞	4. imbalance *n.* 不平衡
5. fundamental *adj.* 根本的；基本的	6. urban *n.* 都市
7. rural *n.* 鄉村	8. urban-rural gap *n.* 城鄉差距

文法應用解析、深入應用補一補

❶ This problem can be solved by increasing the supply of road space or reducing the demand for peak-hour automotive travel.

解析

"This problem can be solved by"（這個問題可以以/被什麼什麼解決），是一個很實用的表達法；by 後面加解決方式。

其它應用

This problem can be solved by adding capacity to bus-only lanes.（這個問題可以以增加公車專用道的容量的方式解決。）

❷ For this reason, I believe narrowing the urban-rural gap is a radical solution in the long run.

解析

這個片語應用在要提供理由時，它是介系詞片語，作副詞用，修飾整句。

其它應用

For this reason, I believe we should improve alternative transportation options（基於這個理由，我相信我們應該改善替代交通工具的選擇。）

3-6 資源回收現況以及其重要性

｜應用句型｜
or、otherwise
或者、否則……

｜搭配口說主題｜
資源回收現況以及其重要性

重點文法搶先看

① 首先；第一：to start with 等

② 也許：perhaps

③ 畢竟：After all, ...

④ 否則：or、otherwise

重要句型與文法放大鏡

① **首先；第一：to start with; to begin with; first of all; in the first place; in the beginning; 相反詞：finally 最後**

To start with, we need to increase the recycling of rubbish because we cannot continue to landfill or burn it forever.（首先，我們必須要增加回收垃圾，因為我們不能永遠繼續做掩埋和把它們燒掉。）

② **也許：perhaps**

Perhaps, at household level, we can use fewer wrapping paper for presents. They can still look good when we reduce the garbage.（或許，在家戶層面，我們可以用更少的包裝紙來包裝禮物。當我們減少垃圾的同時，它們仍然可以看起來很好。）

③ **畢竟：After all, ...**

After all, we only have one Earth. We should do everything to prevent it from becoming a large waste field.（畢竟，我們只有一個地球。我們應該要做任何事，以避免它變得一個大型廢棄物廠。）

④ **否則：or、otherwise**

We have to recycle batteries and electronics, or they will emit pollutants while buried in the landfills. This is because batteries are made from many different chemicals such as lithium-ion.（我們必須回收電池和電子產品，否則，當被埋在掩埋場時，它們會放射出污染物。這是因為電池是從很多不同的化學物質，像是鋰離子做成的。）

文法和口說應用大結合

以上文法和句型可以運用到 IBT、NEW TOEIC 及 IELTS 考試上面，以下列的題目舉例 Track 18

Do you think recycling is necessary? How important is recycling?

你認為回收有其必要嗎？回收有多重要呢？

高分範文

Speaking of recycling, I am very proud to say that Taiwan does a thorough job in recycling; we deal with all sorts of waste including packaging, food, clothes, electronics, batteries and end of life vehicles. We even turn waste into gold. I will explain that in a minute.

說到資源回收，我很驕傲的說，台灣在回收上做得很徹底。我們處理各種的廢棄物包括：包裝、食物、衣服、電子產品、電池，還有廢棄車輛。我們甚至把垃圾變黃金。我待會會解釋這一點。

There are several reasons for recycling. First of all, we are running out places for landfill; the amount of rubbish is

回收基於以下的理由：首先，我們已經沒有地方做掩埋場了。垃圾的數量一直隨著人口

increasing with the growth of population. Most importantly, the earth resource is definitely not unlimited; once it is all used, it is gone forever, such as some mining materials: oil, coal, gold, etc. Therefore, we cannot wait to recycle; otherwise, the Earth is doomed to exhaustion.

成長在增加。更重要的是，地球的資源不是無止境的，一旦用盡，永遠就再也回不來了，像是一些礦產物質：油，煤，金等。因此，回收不能等待，否則地球注定要耗竭。

The ways to reduce rubbish include reducing buying, recycling and reusing. There should be some regulations on labelling symbols on products to provide **consumers** with information about recycling the products. Also, the governments should educate people how to recycle and raise public awareness of the severity of the exhaustion of global resource.

減少垃圾的方法包括：減少購買回收和再使用。應該要有對在產品上和包裝上標籤符號的管制，以提供消費者關於回收這個產品的資訊。而且，政府應該教育民眾如何回收，並且提高民眾地球資源耗竭的嚴重性的意識。

Some Taiwanese companies have **devoted** research and

一些台灣的公司已經致力於研究和發展，

development to turning garbage into something useful, such as building materials. Techniques have been developed to turn plastic bottles into fibers for clothes. In short, we don't want our Earth to become a huge garbage field, so people need to start recycling if they haven't already.

把垃圾變成有用的東西，像是建築材料。一些公司已經發展了把塑膠瓶變成布料用的纖維的技術。簡而言之，我們不想讓我們的地球變成一個巨大的垃圾場，所以如果有人還沒有開始回收，他們需要開始了。

關鍵單字解密

1. sort *n.* 種類	2. electronics *n.* 電子產品
3. doom *v.* 注定	4. consumer *n.* 消費者
5. devote *v.* 致力於	6. technique *n.* 技術

文法應用解析、深入應用補一補

❶ Most importantly, the earth resource is definitely not unlimited.

解析

Most importantly 是副詞片語，修飾一整個句子是在前面列舉幾個事情的嚴重性之後，再指名最嚴重的事情。

其它應用

Items for recycling deal with all sorts of waste, including packaging, electronics, batteries and end of life vehicles. **Most importantly**, it is necessary to recycle batteries because they emit pollutants while buried in the landfills.（回收的項目處理所有種類的廢棄物，包括包裝、電子、電池和廢棄車輛。最重要的是，要回收電池，因為它們會在掩埋場時，放出釋放出污染物。）

❷ We cannot wait to recycle; **otherwise** the Earth is doomed to exhaustion.

解析

otherwise 是副詞，表示 under other circumstances（在別的狀況之下），也就是否則，做語意上的連結。

其它應用

Now the waste of plastic products are floating around the ocean, killing over a million sea birds and large numbers of mammals and turtles each year. We should immediately cut down the use of them. **Otherwise**, the situation will get worse.（現塑膠廢棄物正漂浮在海洋，每年殺死了超過 1 百萬隻的海鳥和很多的哺乳動物和海龜。我們應該立刻減少使用塑膠產品。否則，這個情況會變得更糟。）

4-1 家庭／學校／社會教育

｜以下列的題目舉例｜

- **Which one is more important, family education or school education?** 家庭教育或是學校教育哪一個比較重要？
- **The influence of family/parents/school/society on children's education.** 談家庭／父母親／學校／社會對孩子教育的影響。
- **Freedom to the media or censorship on the media?** 媒體自由或媒體審查。（Ch1 1-5）

❶ **表達個人的想法的重要句型為：**Personally, I would say

解析 1 "Personally"，就個人也可言。"I would say (that)..." 此句型是比較客氣的說法，意思等同：「如果你問我意見，我會這麼說。」

應用 1.1 Personally, I would say our government should increase censorship against the media. (Ch1 1-5)（就個人而言，我會說政府應該對媒體審查。《節選自 Ch1 1-5》）

應用 1.2 Personally, I would say family education is more important than school education. The main reason is that family is the first unit that people encounter in their life. Therefore, family surely has a fundamental influence on individuals.（就個人而言，我會說家庭教育比學校教育更重要。主要理由是，家庭是人們在人生當中所遇到的第一個單位。因此，家庭的確對個人有很根本的影響。）

❷ **表達個人的想法的其它可替換說法：**In my opinion, I would say (that)⋯.

解析 2 opinion 是意見的意思。In my opinion 意思是以我的想法、以我之見，也就是表達個人的意見。

應用 2.1 In my opinion, I would say that every newspaper has its own political agenda. (Ch1 1-2)（以我之見，我會說每家報紙都有自己的政治立場。《節選自 Ch1 1-2》）

應用 2.2 In my opinion, I would say school education is more important. This may sound cruel, but not every parent knows how to be a good parent. School education then plays an extremely crucial part in such cases.（以我之見，學校教育更重要。接下來我要說的可能很殘酷：不是每位父母親都知道如何做好的父母親。此時學

校教育就扮演了特別重要的角色。)

❸ **給理由的重要句型：**The main reason is that＋子句

解析 3 除了用 “because” 來「給理由」之外，想拿高分的英文說法有：“The main reason is＋that＋子句”（主要理由是⋯⋯）。**注意：我們在** Be **動詞之後用是** “that” **而非** “because”。

應用 3.1 The main reason is that paper books would be forgotten and abandoned by children, because they may be far less attractive to them. (Ch1 1-1)（主要的原因是紙本書籍可能會被小孩遺忘或是遺棄，因為它們可能很不吸引孩子。《節選自 Ch1 1-1》）

應用 3.2 The main reason is that schools may not have as fundamental an influence as parents do. However, schools can help students who have difficult family situations.（主要理由是學校可能不如家長有根本的影響力。然而，學校可以幫助來自困難家庭的學生。）

❹ **給理由的重要句型**：First of all、Firstly、First、in the first place（首先、第一點……）

解析 4 在提供自己認為…… 的論點之後，你必須進一步解釋原因。第一點原因可用 First of all、Firstly、First、in the first place 這些片語來起頭。

應用 4.1 It would be dangerous if virtual materials replace printed books. **First of all**, children would lose interest in learning from paper books when they are obsessed by the abundant sound and visual effects of online materials. (Ch1 1-1)（首先，當孩子們著迷于網路材料豐富的聲光效果時，他們會失去從紙本書籍上學習的興趣。《節選自 Ch1 1-1》）

應用 4.2 I believe school education is much more important than family education. **First of all**, parents definitely have an impact on their children's academic achievement.（我相信學校教育遠比家庭教育更重要。首先，父母親絕對能影響他們孩子的學術成就。（Much 修飾比較級。））

❺ **給理由的重要句型**：Second、Secondly、in the second place、third、thirdly、in the third place

解析 5 接下來的第二個論點就可以用 Second、Secondly、in the second place 這些片語來開頭。第三點可以用 third、thirdly、in the third place 來開頭。

應用 5.1 Second, prolonged spending time on the computer or other electronic devices deteriorates eye sight. Third, the information is not always true on the Net. (Ch1 1-1)（第二，經久花時間在電腦或是其他的電子設備上會損害視力。第三，在網路上的訊息並不總是真實的。《節選自 Ch1 1-1》）

應用 5.2 Secondly, parents have more power over their children's education than schools do. Thirdly, habit formation usually starts at early age; once it is formed, schools cannot do much about changing it.（第二、父母親比學校有更多的力量掌管孩子的教育。第三、習慣的形成通常開始於幼年時；一旦形成，學校不能改變它太多。）

❻ 結論句的重要句型：These are some of the reasons that ...

解析 6 論述完畢之前，要有結尾，通常一句話就可以，如：These are some of the reasons that...（這些就是一些……的原因）。或 These are the reasons that…（以上就是我……的理由）。**提點** 記得理由可不能只給一個喔！所以要用複數—These are reasons（reasons 要加 s！）。如果你實在只有一個理由的話，只好用：This is the（main）reason that... 「這就是（主要的）原因（單數）」，或者是：This is one of the reasons that... 「這就是原因之一」的句型來表達。

應用 6.1 These are some of the reasons that I don't agree that children should use the Internet when they are too young. (Ch1 1-1)（這些是我不贊成小孩在太早的年紀使用網路的原因。《節選自 Ch1 1-1》）

應用 6.2 These are some of the reasons that I believe parenting is more important than school education.（以上就是我認為父母的管教比學校教育重要的理由。）

4-2 風俗文化

｜以下列的題目舉例｜

- **Talk about your culture. What's unique about it?** 談論你們的文化。有什麼獨特之處？
- **What are the advantages and disadvantages of private schools and public/state schools?** 私立學校和公立學校的優勢和劣勢（Ch2 2-1）
- **Describe your hometown/country: today and the past.** 請談談你的家鄉／國家：現在與過去（Ch3 3-1）
- **Current environmental issues and solutions** 現在的環境問題和解決方案（Ch3 3-3）

❶ **要求作兩者之間比較，以：**“Well, let me start with…” or “ to start with,... ” 開始。

解析 1 談文化經常要作比較，當你被要求作兩者之間比較，你可以由：“Well, let me start with…” 開始。well 是發語詞，“Let me….”是祈使句，祈使句是表示請求、命令、勸告或禁止等語氣的句子。由於此類句型都是用來跟眼前的人（You）說話，所以通常省略主詞，You。因為原本的句型中的主詞是第二人稱，所以動詞也就是同原形動詞。“Well, let me start with…”就是「好的，讓我先......」。

應用 1.1 Well, let me start with private schools. (Ch2 2-1)
（好的，讓我先從私立學校開始。《節選自 Ch2 2-1》）

應用 1.2 Well, to start with, I'd like to talk about the unique features of Taiwanese culture.（好的，首先我想要談介紹台灣文化獨特的特點。）

❷ **表達有其他理由、論點的重要說法：** besides, along with... ,

解析 2 "Besides"，是介系詞，意思是「此外、還有」。"along with" 後面加名詞再加逗點加上主要子句

應用 2.1 Besides, the 24 hour convenience stores, such as 7-11, are everywhere and sell almost everything. (Ch3 3-1)
（24 小時的便利商店，像是 7-11，到處都有，幾乎什麼東西都有賣。《節選自 Ch3 3-1 》）

應用 2.2 Along with gift giving etiquette, we have dining etiquette to be careful about. For example, you need to dress well to give face to your hosts.（除了給送禮的禮節之外，我們有用餐禮儀也是需要注意的。譬如，你需要注重穿著，以給主人面子。）

③ 表明因果的重要說法：As a result, as a consequence... .

解析 3 as a result, as a consequence 介詞片語做副詞，翻作「結果」、「因此」，用以連接句意上的前一句因，而後一句是果。

應用 3.1 As a result, students' particular academic needs and weaknesses are easier noticed by teachers. (Ch2 2-1)（結果，學生在學業上有特別的需要或是弱點，都可以比較容易被老師注意到。《節選自 Ch2 2-1》）

應用 3.2 The cultural preference of male descendants was dominant. As a consequence, parents preferred a boy to a girl.（在過去在文化上偏好男性子孫是主導性的看法。因此，家長們偏好男孩，而不是女孩。）

應用 3.3 In 1895, China was defeated in the Sino-Japanese War. As a consequence, Taiwan was ceded to Japan and colonised for 50 years.（在 1895 年，中國在中日戰爭戰敗；結果，台灣就被割讓給日本，並且自此被殖民五十年。）

④ **作比較的重要說法**：In contrast, in comparison to, unlike

解析 4 In contrast, in comparison to, unlike 都是「對照之下」、「與……成對比」，都是用來對比兩件事或兩個人之不同處。

應用 4.1 ... it is well-known that their tuition fees are hugely expensive, which is the major drawback. In contrast, public schools are more affordable,... (Ch2 2-1)（眾所周知的是他們巨量昂貴的學費，這就是最大的缺點。對照之下，公立學校比較付得起……《節選自 Ch2 2-1》）

*此例是作 private school 和 public schools 兩者之間的比較

應用 4.2 In comparison to the past, the birth rate in Taiwan has reduced steadily. Increased education and delayed marriages reduce the potential of females aged between 20 and 30 to become a mother.（與過去作比較，台灣的出生率已經穩定的下降。教育提高和晚婚減少 20 至 30 歲的女士成為母親的可能性。）

*此例是作 the past 和 now（由 has reduced 知道）兩者之間的比較

⑤ 即使儘管的重要句型：though, although, even though

解析 5 even though 和 although 兩者都是雖然、儘管的意思，但 even though 意思更強烈。Although 和 Though 兩者都是雖然、儘管的意思，而兩者區別僅在於 though 較不正式。

應用 5.1 Though the climate is generally pleasant, there are on average three to four typhoons that hit Taiwan every year. (Ch3 3-1)（雖然天氣一般來說都是很愉悅的，但是台灣一年有三到四個颱風侵襲。《節選自 Ch3 3-1》）

應用 5.2 Even though many Taiwanese don't have formal religious belief, they engage in religious practices, such as burning incense to worship a deity, hero or ancestor at home, or visiting a temple to wish good luck for exams.（即使很多台灣人沒有正式的宗教信仰，他們也從事宗教性的活動，像是在家燒香崇拜神、英雄或是祖先，或是到廟裡為考試請求好運。）

⑥ 結論句的重要說法：結論、總之 To conclude; In conclusion,

解析 6 conclude（結論）是動詞，它的名詞是 conclusion；做結論的時候，可以用 “to conclude” 這一個不定詞片語，或是介系詞片語 “in conclusion” 做副詞，修飾整句。

應用 6.1 To conclude, unless we address these issues seriously, disasters and tragedies are bound to happen soon and in the future. (Ch3 3-3)（結論是，除非我們正視這些嚴肅的問題，否則災難和悲劇是注定要即將和在未來發生的。《適用於 Ch3 3-3》）

應用 6.2 To conclude, Confucian thinking is still deep-rooted in Taiwanese culture.（總之，儒家思想在台灣文化仍然根深蒂固。）

應用 6.3 Inconclusion, Taoism, folk culture and superstition prevail in Taiwan.（總之，道教，民俗文化和迷信盛行於台灣。）

4-3

談能源危機

｜以下列的題目舉例｜

- **People are aware of global energy crises. What are those crises and what are the solutions to them?** 人們已經意識到了全球的能源危機。全球的能源危機有哪些？有什麼解決辦法？
- **traffic problems and solutions** 交通問題和建議解決辦法（Ch3 3-4）
- **current environmental issues and solutions** 環境問題和解決方案（Ch3 3-2）
- **Do you think recycling necessary? How important is recycling?** 你認為回收有其必要嗎？回收有多重要呢？（Ch3 3-6）

❶ **表「一般來說」的重要說法：**generally speaking,...; in general

解析 1 "generally speaking"（一般來說）是獨立分詞構句，兩個原句中，兩個主詞是不同的，因此通常主詞不可以省略。但是主詞是不特定的人，就可以省略。

應用 1.1 Generally speaking, traffic problems in big cities include too many automobiles, too narrow of roads and streets and too few parking spaces. (Ch3 3-4)（一般來說，在大都市的交通問題是車輛太多、道路和街道太窄，以及停車位太少。《節選自 Ch3 3-4》

應用 1.2 Generally speaking, energy crises, including natural resource depletion, food and water shortage, have become a serious concern, and should be dealt with immediately.（一般來說，能源危機包括自然資源的用盡、食物和水的短缺，已經成為令人嚴肅擔心的事情，並且應該要立刻的處理。）

❷ **修飾數量很多的形容詞** A great deal of/number of

解析 2 "A great deal" 是修飾不可數名詞的數量形容詞；"a great number of"是修飾可數名詞的數量形容詞，"a lot of"="lots of" 兩種名詞都可以用。

應用 2.1 The automobiles generate a great deal of exhaust and this results in air pollution. (Ch3 3-4)（車輛產生大量的廢氣，因此導致空氣污染。《節選自 Ch3 3-4》）

應用 2.2 Human beings consume a great deal of meat every year, twice as much as we did 30 years ago.

Thus, people need to breed a great number of animals. Those animals need vast amounts of food and water, emit methane and other greenhouse gases and produce physical waste.（人類每年消耗大量的肉，比我們 30 年前的消耗是兩倍之多。因此，人們需要養大量的動物。這些動物需要大量的水和食物、排放甲烷、還有其他溫室氣體，並產生很多排泄物。）

❸ 表示絕對的重要副詞：undoubtedly, surely, certainly

解析 3 可以看出 undoubtedly（無疑地），surely（的確是），certainly（一定是）這些副詞的意思很強烈，所以，後面你必須要接很強而有力的證據，來支持你的論點。

應用 3.1 Undoubtedly, global warming has become top of the list which requires urgent attention. (Ch3 3-2)（無庸置疑的，全球暖化已經是在名單的首位，需要迫切的注意。《節選自 Ch3 3-2》）

應用 3.2 Although not many people are aware of the damage that fast food, plastic, packaging and cheap electronics can cause, undoubtedly, their wastes threaten the well-being of humans.（雖然不是很多人都意識到速食、塑膠、包裝和廉價的電子產品所帶的損害；但是

無疑地，它們的廢棄物威脅到人類的福祉。）

應用 3.3 Global population growth certainly helps to accelerate the exhaustion of natural resources and cause energy crises.（全球人口增加的確加速自然資源的耗竭，並且引起能源危機。）

❹ 表示否則的重要的字：otherwise, or

解析 4 注意 “or” 是連接詞，但 “otherwise” 不是連接詞，是副詞作用，不能連接子句。

應用 4.1 We cannot wait to recycle; otherwise, the Earth is doomed to exhaustion. (Ch3 3-6)（回收不能等待，否則地球注定要耗竭。《節選自 Ch3 3-6》）

應用 4.2 People argue that the use of genetically engineered plants should be increased, as a fuel alternative to gasoline; otherwise, there will not be power to drive machines and vehicles soon.（人們主張應該要增加基因改造植物的使用，以作為汽油的替代燃料；否則很快就沒有燃料以驅動機器和汽車。）

應用 4.3 We shouldn't depend on genetically modified

food as a solution to food shortage, or we are taking a great risk of altering the balance of ecological systems.（我們不應該依靠基因改造食品，作為食物短缺的解決方案，否則，我們是正在冒改變生態平衡的重大風險。）

⑤ **表示如果這（論點）是真的**：if this is the case, if this is true

解析 5 if this is the case,用來表示你之前的推論如果是事實的話接下來會發生什麼樣的結果。

應用 5.1 This may be caused by the fact that cars are so cheap. If this is the case, governments should levy higher taxes on private vehicles and raise the price of gasoline in order to discourage the use of private vehicles.(Ch3 3-4)

（這個原因可能是汽車太便宜的事實導致的。如果這是事實的話，政府應該要在私人的交通工具上徵收更高的稅，並且提高汽油的成本，以為抑制購買和使用私人交通工具。《節選自 Ch3 3-4》）

應用 5.2 According to some research, nuclear waste disposal has tremendous health hazards associated with it. If this is the case, nuclear power plants should be banned.（根據一些研究，核能廢棄物牽連到巨大的健康危害。如果這是事實的話，核能發電廠應該被禁止。）

應用 5.3 If nuclear waste resulting in genetic mutation is the case, efforts must be made to develop renewable sources of energy, such as solar, wind, biogas and geothermal energy.（如果核能廢棄物會導致基因突變的話，我們必須對發展再生能源，像是太陽能、風能、生物氣體和地熱能，付出更大的努力。）

⑥ **表達「總的來說」的重要說法**：by and large; on the whole; all in all; everything considered

解析 6 這些都是表示總的來說，做結論的方法。

應用 6.1 By and large, traffic problems are too serious to neglect. (Ch3 3-4)（大致說來，交通問題是太嚴重了，以至於無法忽略。《節選自 Ch3 3-4》）

應用 6.2 All in all, the simplest and cheapest thing anyone can do is to eat less meat.（總之，任何人可以做的最簡單和最便宜的方式就是，減少吃肉。）

4-4

科技與科學

| 以下列的題目舉例 |

- **Do students in the classroom have a better learning experience than online students?** 在教室學習的學生，會比網路學習的學生，有更好的學習經驗嗎？
- **Co-ed or single-sex schools?** 男女合校或是分校？（Ch2 2-6）
- **Comment on the common pathways for students to go to university** 評論進入大學的管道（Ch2 2-3）
- **Describe pathways for a student to go to university** 描述進入大學的管道（Ch2 2-2）
- **the educational systems and suggestions** 教育系統與建議（Ch2 2-4）

❶ **表優勢和劣勢的說法：某事物** has its pros and cons; the advantages and disadvantages of **某事物**

解析 1 這二句型常用來表達某事物的優缺點，或對照比較兩事物的優勢和劣勢。

應用 1.1 Surely both types of schools have their pros and cons. (Ch2 2-6)（的確兩種學校都各有他們的優缺點。《節選自（Ch2 2-6）》

應用 1.2 Both classroom and online learning have their pros and cons.（教室和網路學習兩者，都有它們的優勢和劣勢。）

❷ **作比較的重要句型**：while… ;whereas…

解析 2 很多文法書寫這兩個字和 but（但是）、although / though（雖然）的用法相同，其實並不然，while、whereas 的重點是在用來對照比較的兩者之間不同處，中文可以翻作「而」。它們是附屬連接詞用來連接兩個子句。

應用 2.1 ... a gifted and intelligent child can thrive and succeed in any school, while a less intelligent child may benefit from the extra academic attention at private school. (Ch2 2-1)（有天份和聰明的孩子在任何學校都可以蓬勃發展，而較不聰明的孩子可以在私立學校，因為學業上受到特別的重視而獲益。《節選自（Ch2 2-1）》）

應用 2.2 Whereas larger class sizes in the traditional classroom usually limit the opportunity to interact, the online classroom provides the opportunity to participate, without the pressure of a limited time or speaking in front of a group.（當傳統教室較大的班級人數通常限制了互動的機會，而網路教室提供沒有時間限制的壓力，也沒有在

小組前面發言的壓力的參與機會。）

❸「以／就…而言」，「以…來看（一件事／物）」的重要說法：In terms of, regarding, in relation to

解析 3 regarding, in relation to 是介系詞片語，後面加名詞或是 ving；“regarding”、“in relation to” 是與什麼有關聯的意思。與“In terms of,”同，也表示「以／就…而言」，「以…來看（一件事／物）」。

應用 3.1 In terms of fairness, I prefer the traditional Entrance Exams to admission by application.(Ch2 2-3)（就公平性而言，和申請入學比較，我偏好傳統的入學考試。《節選自（Ch2 2-3）》）

應用 3.2 Regarding attractiveness to learners, I would say that a really good teacher can make traditional classrooms as exciting as the online classroom.（就對學習者的吸引力而言，我會說一位真正好的老師，能夠讓傳統的教室和網路教室一樣的令人興奮。）

應用 3.3 In relation to emotional support and immediate feedback, online classroom as well as traditional classrooms can allow that to happen.（就情緒和立即的回

饋而言，網路教室能和傳統教室一樣，也可以做得到。）

❹ as long as（**只要**）；unless（**除非**），**取代** if **的用法**：

解析 4 as long as; unless 這兩個詞可取代 if，所以也是用假設語氣

應用 4.1 You can enter any university of your desire as long as your scores meet their requirements. (Ch2 2-2)（你可以進入你想要唸的大學，只要你的分數達到他們的要求。《節選自（Ch2 2-2）》*此例句 Type 0 是條件句，已在 Ch2 2-3 介紹。）

應用 4.2 Traditional classrooms can be as exciting as the online classroom as long as/if the teacher is very skilful.（只要老師非常有技巧，傳統的教室可以和網路教室一樣令人興奮。）

應用 4.3 I don't agree with using online learning unless it can also allow immediate feedback and interaction between instructor and learners.（我不同意使用網路教學，除非它可以有的立即的回饋，及老師和學生之間的互動。）

❺ **表示「更糟的是」的重要說法**：To make it worse, to make matters worse

解析 5 "To make it worse,"，"to make matters worse,"是不定詞片語，作副詞用，修飾整個句子。worse 是 bad 的比較級。

應用 5.1 To make it worse, exams only took place once a year. (Ch2 2-3)（糟糕的是，這個考試一年只考一次。《節選自（Ch2 2-3）》）

應用 5.2 Larger class sizes not only restrict interaction between students but also reduce the attention which individual students can receive from the teacher. To make matters worse, the teacher makes boring tedious lectures.（班級人數較多，不僅限制了學生之間的互動，也減少了個別學生可以獲得老師的注意力。當老師無聊又冗長地講課時，這情況更糟。）

應用 5.3 To make matters worse, it frustrates students when the teachers are defeated by technology issues.（更糟的是，當老師被技術上的問題打敗時，學生會感到挫折。）

⑥ **把某人或某事列入考慮的重要說法**：To take 某人／某事 into consideration,... ; bearing 某人／某事 in mind

解析 6 "To take 某人／某事 into consideration," 就是它字面上的意思；"bearing sth. in mind" 是 "I would like you to bear in mind" 的分詞構句。

應用 6.1 To take these drawbacks into consideration, I strongly propose traditional entrance exams remain and be held twice a year. (Ch2 2-4)（考慮了這些缺點，我提議傳統的入學考試應該維持，並且一年舉辦兩次。《節選自（Ch2 2-4）》）

應用 6.2 Bearing these factors in mind, teachers cannot entirely depends on technology in teaching.（把這些因素考慮進去的話，老師不可以完全的依賴科技在教學上。）

4-5 環境議題：以科技發展為例

｜以下列的題目舉例｜

- **The benefits of technology far outweigh the disadvantages. Do you agree or disagree? Explain your reasons by using specific details.** 科技的好處遠超過於它的壞處。你同意或是不同意？請以特定的細節來解釋你的理由。
- **Current urgent environmental issues and provide solutions.** 目前急迫的環境問題與解決方案（Ch3 3-2）
- **Environmental issues and people's responsibilities** 環境問題與人類的責任（Ch3 3-3）
- **Recommendations for reducing traffic congestion?** 對解決塞車之建議（Ch3 3-5）

❶ **不可否認的**：There is no denying that... .

解析 1 deny（否認）是動詞；There is no denying that 用來表示某事是絕對的，後面加 that 子句。

應用 1.1 There is no denying that our environment is constantly changing.(Ch3 3-2)（不可否認的，我們的環境一直不斷的在改變。《適用於（Ch3 3-2）》）

應用 1.2 There is no denying that the inventions of vehicles and airplanes make travel much easier, and consequently save a lot of effort and time.（不可否認的是，汽車和飛機的發明，使得旅遊方便許多，伴隨而來節省很多精力和時間。）

❷ **表達「還有」「更者」**：furthermore, moreover, what is more

解析 2 furthermore, moreover, what is more 是要提供更多看法的轉折語，用來預告（signal）將提供其他的論點。

應用 2.1 Furthermore, countries should develop agreements signed by multiple governments to prevent damage or manage the impacts of human activity on natural resources. (Ch3 3-3)（進一步的，更多國家之間應該發展協議，多國國家共同簽署，以避免損害或是管理人類活動對自然資源的影響。《節選自（Ch3 3-3）》）

應用 2.2 Technology, such as the internet, communication tools and software, makes family and friends closer. **Moreover**, it makes business easier and more efficient.

（科技，像是網路和溝通工具和軟體，使得家庭和朋友更接近。更者，它使商業活動可以進行得更容易和更有效率。）

❸ 表達「儘管」、「雖然」：despite, ;in spite of

解析 3 despite, in spite of 兩者是介系詞，後面要接名詞或是動名詞。

應用 3.1 **Despite** these severe environmental issues, the global warming crisis has not been controlled effectively, and neither has the population explosion. (Ch3 3-2)（全球暖化危機並沒有被有效的控制，環境人口爆炸也沒有，儘管這些環境問題很嚴重。《適用於（Ch3 3-2）》）

應用 3.2 Nuclear power is an alternative to natural sources of energy, with less cost yet more effective in generating energy. **Despite** its merits, people cannot neglect the risks it can cause.（雖然核能發電是自然能源的替代方式，較少的成本，但是更有效率。儘管這些優點，人們還是不能忽遠它可能造成的風險。）

應用 3.3 Taking the inventions of weapons for example, **in spite of** helping countries to defeat enemies, but at the same time, they kill people on a large scale and often in the blink of an eye.（以武器的發明舉例，雖然幫助國家打勝仗，但是同時間它們大規模的殺人無數，通常在眨眼之間，就可以辦到。）

❹ **表達「換言之」**：that is,; in other words

解析 4 that is, in other words 用來表示描述同一件事實的另一個說法，也就是「換言之」，它們不是連接詞，如果不另外用連接詞的話，可以用分號連接兩個句子。

應用 4.1 The damage caused by such human activities is aggravated by another severe current environmental problem; that is, overpopulation. (Ch3 3-2)（另外一個因人類活動而造成當前嚴重的環境問題，就是人口過盛的問題而加劇了。《節選自（Ch3 3-2）》）

應用 4.2 People can use guns to protect themselves. However, they can also be misused by robbers organgsters; in other words, they can be used for malice and cause fatalities.（人們可以使用槍枝來保護他們自己，然而，它們也可能被強盜和歹徒錯誤的使用；也就是，它們可以被惡意使用，變得致命。）

❺ 表達「「簡而言之」：in short, in brief

解析 5 short, brief 兩者都是形容詞，in short, in brief（簡而言之），長話短說的意思，也可是「總而言之」，做歸納結論使用。

應用 5.1 In short, environmental protection should be done at all individual, organizational and governmental levels. (Ch3 3-3)（簡而言之，為了自然環境和人類，環境保護應該在個人、機構和政府的層面都要做到。《節選自（Ch3 3-3）》）

應用 5.2 In brief, the technology in travelling tools makes life more convenient, but at the same time, those tools emit excess amounts of carbon footprint, resulting in environmental crises.（簡而言之，交通工具上的科技使生活變得更方便，但是同時，這些工具排放過量的碳足跡，導致環境危機。）

❻「基於這個理由」：For this reason; for these reasons, in these circumstances, therefore

解析 6 「基於這個理由」只有一個理由時，使用單數 "For this reason,"，"in this circumstance,"；不只有一個理由時，名詞和指示形容詞換成複數："For these reasons,"，"in these circumstances," 它們是系詞片語，作副詞用，以修飾整個句子。

應用 6.1 For this reason, I believe narrowing the urban-rural gap is a radical solution in the long run. (Ch3 3-5)（基於這個理由，我相信縮小城鄉差距還是在長期根本的辦法。《節選自（Ch3 3-5）》）

應用 6.2 It is often the case that people use technology for evil intention. In these circumstances, I believe the disadvantages of technology far outweigh the advantages.（人們使用科技在做壞事上面是經常有的事。在這些情況之下，我相信科技的壞處是遠超過它的好處的。）

4-6 學校生活：談學生追求名牌為例

｜以下列的題目舉例｜

- **Nowadays, students have changed from meeting their basic needs to pursuing brand names for their clothes and accessories. Do you think this phenomenon should be discouraged or it is nothing to worry about? Explain your reasons with supporting details.** 今日，學生從滿足他們對衣服和附屬品的基本需要，到追求名牌。你認為這是必須遏止的現象，或是不用擔心呢？請解釋你的理由。
- **School experience** 談學校的經驗（Ch2 2-5）
- **Comment the common pathways for students to go to university** 評論進入大學的管道（Ch2 2-3）
- **Describe pathways for a student to go to university** 描述進入大學的管道（Ch2 2-2）
- **the educational systems and suggestions** 教育系統與建議（Ch2 2-4）
- **The advantages and disadvantages of private and public schools** 私立學校和公立學校的優勢和劣勢（Ch2 2-1）

❶ **表達仔細考慮**：think about; **擔心**：worry about

解析 1 think about（仔細考慮），worry about（擔心），注意介系詞用 “about”

應用 1.1 This is because without their participation, there would be nothing to think about and no way of understanding what is read or observed. (C2 2-5)（這是因為沒有參與，就沒有思考，也就沒有了解他們所讀的或是觀察到的。《節選自（Ch2 2-5）》）

應用 1.2 Well, for students wanting brand names, it is nothing to worry about.（好的，對於學生追求名牌，這並不需要擔心。

❷ **介紹事情有幾種途徑／類型／方法的起頭用**：There are two common pathways/types/methods/ways to do sth.

解析 2 一般有兩種途徑／類型／方法來做某件事情以：There are two common pathways（途徑）／types（類型）／methods/ways（方法）to do sth. 起頭。

應用 2.1 There are two common pathways for students to go to university. (Ch2 2-3)（有兩種常見的入大學方式。《節選自（Ch2 2-3）》）

應用 2.2 There are two common reactions when their parents don't satisfy their material needs: complaining or trying hard to get what they want.（對他們的父母不滿

足他們的物質需要，通常有兩種反應：抱怨或是設法得到他們所想要的。)

❸ 連綴動詞 become（變成、成為）

解析 3 連綴動詞是一組特殊動詞，需加上形容詞（*非副詞）或名詞，以使語意完整。

應用 3.1 In the past, there used to be only one pathway to university, which was to pass the National University Entrance Exams. Now it has **become** an alternative. (Ch2 2-2)（在過去只有一個進入大學的方式，就是通過國家大學入學考試。現在它已經變成一種選擇方式。《節選自（Ch2 2-2）》）

應用 3.2 In the first case, students are not financially independent; they spend their parents' hard-earned money. If this **becomes** a habit, once their parents stop the supply, they complain.（第一個情況，學生並在財務上並沒有獨立；他們花他們父母的辛苦錢。如果就成為了習慣，一旦他們的父母停止供給，他們就抱怨。)

④ **使人…做…**：make; have; let; help

解析 4 make; have; let; help 是另一組特殊動詞——使役動詞，表叫…去做…；讓…去…做；使人去…做…。主要有三種：make, have, let, 當有第二個動詞，直接加，不加 to, “help”也是使役動詞，但加不加“to”都可以。

應用 4.1 Teachers cannot **make** learning happen but can only influence its focus, speed and direction. (Ch2 2-5)（老師們不能讓學習發生，但是能夠影響學習的焦點、速度和方向。《節選自（Ch2 2-5）》）

應用 4.2 Also, some students wear expensive items to school, and this may **make** students who are not as rich **feel** bad, even **lower** their self-esteem.（此外，一些學生穿著昂貴的物品到學校，這可能使沒有那麼有錢的學生，感到不舒服，甚至貶低他們的自尊。）

應用 4.3 Some classmates or schoolmates, whether they are rich or not, compare the value of their clothes or accessories, and this **makes** the focus on schooling less strong.（一些同班同學或同校的同學，不管他們是否有錢，他們比較他們的衣服或是附件的價值，這造成他們對於學業重視較少。）

⑤ 表示一方面……；另一方面，……：For one thing,…. ；For another,...

解析 5：“For one thing,… . For another,… .”表示一方面…，另一方面，這兩方面是補充的，如果要表示相矛盾的兩個方面，用 “on one hand..., on the other hand... ”。

應用 5.1 For one thing, it does not help reduce the students’ burden. For another, this form can be easier manipulated by people who have power. (Ch2 2-4)（一方面它並沒有幫助減輕學生的負擔。另一方面，這一個形式容易被有權力的人所操縱。《節選自（Ch2 2-4）》）

應用 5.2 For students consuming brand names, for one thing, it may twist students’ values on material things; for another, students may lose the virtue of frugality.（對於學生消費名牌物品，一方面可能會扭曲學生對物質的價值觀；另一方面，學生可能會失去節儉的美德。）

應用 5.3 For one thing, brand items cost much more than normal products. For another, brand names is not a synonym for quality. Students need to be taught that quality is more important in choosing products.（一方面，名牌的花費比一般產品貴了許多，另一方面，名牌並不

是品質的同義詞。學生們應該要被教導品質是在選擇商品時，比較重要的。）

❻ **表示因此；所以的副詞**：therefore; thus; hence

解析 6 therefore; thus; hence, 是副詞，作語義上的連結。

應用 6.1 They tend to be smaller at private schools, and therefore, private schools usually have better teacher-student ratios. (Ch2 2-1)（私立學校的傾向是比較小的班級。因此，私立學校通常有較好的師生比。《節選自（Ch2 2-2）》）

應用 6.2 There are few rationales for students to buy brand names. Thus, I think this phenomenon should be discouraged.（有很少的正當理由支持學生來買名牌。因此，我認為這個現象，應該被遏止。）

將看完的單元打個勾，強效提升D說自信心！

☐ 看完 Chapter 5 連接詞、詞性轉換、時態、社交類題型沒問題！

☐ 搞定 Chapter 6 名詞子句、關係代名詞、邏輯、價值觀類題型通通都會了！

☐ 讀過 Chapter 7 分詞構句、生活旅遊、政府政策類題型 OK！

☐ 複習 Chapter 8 前 3 章總整理與延伸應用，學習印象更深了！

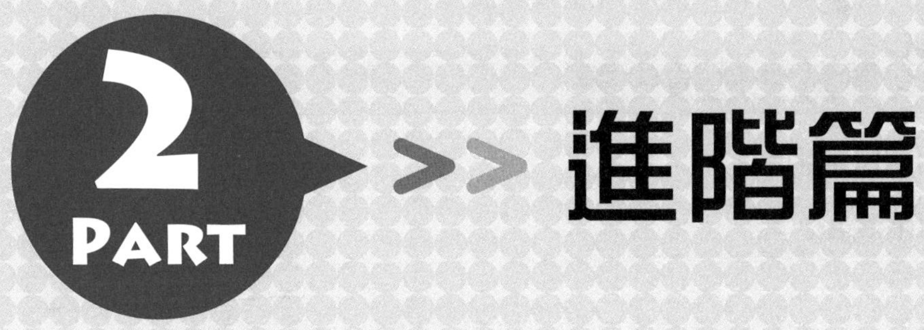

現在進入 **Part 2** 進階篇，學習更多較難的句型！

5-1 談交友、朋友的選擇

應用句型	搭配口說主題
rather than 而不是……	談交友、朋友的選擇

重點文法搶先看

① rather than

② instead

重要句型與文法放大鏡

① **"rather than" 當介係詞「而不是…」，可和 "instead of" 互換，後方需搭配「名詞」或「動名詞」（Ving）。"rather than" 可當連接詞，連接兩個詞性相同的字詞或子句。"rather than" 連接兩個主詞時，動詞需和前面的主詞一致，因為它才是重點。**

例 1 A healthy friendship allows both people to have a reasonable amount of control, rather than one person bossing the other around.（健康的友誼是讓兩人都有合理的控制，而不是都是一人指使另外一個人。）

例 2 When you are making plans or an important decision with a friend, you both should contribute ideas and make choices together, rather than the other person dominating and making all the decisions.（當你和朋友一起做計劃或是重要的決策時，你們兩個人都應該要貢獻想法和一同做選擇，而不都是一個人在支配並且做所有的決定。）

例 3 Many people choose friends whose personality traits are similar to theirs rather than different from.（很多人選擇和自己有相似，而非不同的個人特質當朋友。）

② **"instead" 和 "rather" 當副詞是「而是、反而、卻」，常放在句首或句尾。**

例 1 I don't choose friends; rather, I make friends with whoever makes me feel good about myself.（我不選擇朋友，而是，誰讓我的感受很好，我就跟他做朋友。）

例 2 I don't choose friends based on their looks. Instead, being friendly is more important.（我不基於外觀選擇朋友。而是，友善才是最重要的）

文法和口說應用大結合

以上文法和句型可以運用到 IBT、NEW TOEIC 及 IELTS 考試上面，以下列的題目舉例 Track 19

Tell how often you meet your friends. Explain your reasons. How do you choose friends? Explain your choices.

談你多久和你的朋友見面。請解釋你的理由。你如何選擇朋友的？請解釋你的選擇。

高分範文

Friends are very important to me; therefore, I meet them as frequently as I can. I often meet some friends on the weekend. This allows us more time to relax and have fun together since I work during the week.

朋友對我來說非常重要；因此，我盡可能地經常跟他們見面。我常在週末和我的一些朋友見面。因為我週一到週五上班，這樣子才會有更多的時間來放鬆和一起玩樂。

I choose friends with similar personalities to mine. I think this helps us to get along well.

我選擇和我個性相似的朋友。我認為這能幫助我們相處得很好。

People say you can judge a person by the friends they keep; well, I am a moral person. So, I only make friends with those who have similar morals to me.

俗話說你可以觀其友視其人；我是一個有道德觀念的人。所以我只交和我有相似道德觀念標準的朋友。

One of the most important characteristics of a friend is their ability to be trusted. Finding those that you can rely on is essential in order to form a strong friendship, as you may share secrets and stories with them. You should also be able to count on them for their unconditional support.

其中一個最重要的朋友特點的是，他們可以被信任的能力。為了要建立一段很堅強的友誼，找你可以信賴的人是很重要的，因為你可以和他們分享秘密和故事。你應該也可以依賴他們無條件的支持。

Also, I always choose supportive people. You should find a friend who is willing to support you through difficult situations and always be there for you. Choosing a friend who

此外，我總是選擇會支持我的朋友。你應該找一個願意支持你度過困境，並且總是在那裡支持你的朋友。選擇一個能夠給你可靠建議

gives you reliable advice and their words may have an impact on your choices.

的朋友，他們的話可能對你的選擇有重要的影響。

To me, what really makes a friendship last is someone who is genuine, nice, supportive and easy-going.

對我來說，真誠、善良、夠挺你，又隨和朋友，才是讓友誼長久的因素。

關鍵單字解密

1. count on *v.* 依賴	2. unconditional *adj.* 無條件的

文法應用解析、深入應用補一補

❶ I choose friends with similar personalities to mine.

解析

mine 是所有格代名詞，表示某某人的。所有格代名詞是所有格＋名詞的合體，可以用以下算式表示：**所有格代名詞＝所有格＋名詞** 例：my personalities = mine

人稱	數	主格	所有格	所有格代名詞
第一人稱	單數	I	my	mine
	複數	we	our	ours

第二人稱	單數	you	your	yours
	複數	you	your	yours
第三人稱	單數	he	his	his
		she	her	hers
		it	its	its
	複數	they	their	theirs

其它應用

You should communicate with your friend if his or her ideas are different from **yours**.（如果你的朋友的意見和你的不同，你應該和他/她溝通。）

提點 different 搭配的介系詞用 “from”。

❷ What really makes a friendship last is someone who is genuine, nice, supportive and easy-going.

解析

What 是關係子句＝the thing which；which 是主格的地位。

其它應用

What makes a really good friend is someone who listens, supports and has a good influence on you.（真正的好朋友是願意傾聽、支持和對你有好影響的人。）

5-2 社交活動（偏好的聚會活動及場所）

｜應用句型｜
名詞作形容詞用

｜搭配口說主題｜
社交活動

重點文法搶先看

① **名詞轉換形容詞變化 1**：名詞 N＋ful：表示充滿～的、富有～的

② **名詞轉換形容詞變化 2**：名詞 N＋less：表示少～的，無～的

③ **名詞轉換形容詞變化 3**：名詞 N＋N：以名詞作修飾語——強調內容或職能；以形容詞作修飾語側重屬性和特徵

重要句型與文法放大鏡

形容詞是用來修飾「名詞」，用來表示人和事物的形狀、性質、動作、行為的性質狀態等等。有些形容詞是名詞轉換過來的，整理如下：

① **名詞轉換形容詞**：名詞 N＋ful 表示充滿～的、富有～的；形容詞如：wonderful（很棒的）；cheerful（快樂的）；

meaningful（有意義的），變化如下：

N.	wonder	cheer	meaning	power	joy
Adj	wonderful	cheerful	meaningful	powerful	joyful

例 My friends and I like to hang out at the same pub; we always have a wonderful time there.（我的朋友和我喜歡在同一間酒吧消磨時光；我們總是在那裡過得很愉快。）

② **名詞 N＋less 表示少～的，無～的**；例如：sleepless（沒睡覺的）；endless（無盡的）；valueless（無價值的）；aimless（無目標的），變化如下：

N.	sleep	end	value	aim
Adj.	sleepless	endless	valueless	aimless

例 For people who live in a sleepless city, friends can have a lot of places to hang around even in the middle of the night.（對於住在不夜城的人，朋友們可以有很多的地方消磨時光，甚至在大半夜的時候都有很多地方可以去。）

③ **名詞修飾「名詞」，作形容詞用**：名詞作修飾語時，與同詞根的形容詞或分詞作修飾語，有語意上的差別—不同在：以名詞作修飾語—強調內容或職能；以形容詞作修飾語側重屬性和特徵。以下解釋：health food 指的是保健食品，表示 The food is about health.；而 healthy food 則是健康食

品，表示 The food is healthy.保健食品並非是健康食品（遇到黑心廠商）例：Friends who share special hobbies or interests may organize regular activities, such as band practice, bowling matches, study groups, and so on.（有共同嗜好和興趣的朋友們，可以組織規律的活動，比如樂團練習、保齡球賽、讀書社等等。）

文法和口說應用大結合

以上文法和句型可以運用到 IBT、NEW TOEIC 及 IELTS 考試上面，以下列的題目舉例 Track 20

What do you usually do with your friends? What are the common places for social activities in your country?

你通常和朋友做什麼活動？在你的國家，哪些是一般社交活動的場所？

高分範文

Most of my friends and I share common interests, such as chatting, shopping, and watching TV and movies.

我大部分的朋友和我有共同的興趣，比如聊天、購物、看電視和電影。因此，這些就是

Therefore, these are things I usually do with them.

我通常和他們一起做的事情。

I think those are also common things people do with their friends in Taiwan. Almost every day, you see people sitting in a café chatting, having a drink. Friends shop together at department stores. We also like to hang around in friends' houses We may go to restaurants to socialize and at the same time fill our stomachs. For friends who have special shared hobbies or interests, they may organize regular activities, such as band practice, bowling matches, study groups, and so on. You can also see teenagers wandering around or hanging out aimlessly, or at McDonalds where food and drink is affordable and they offer

我認為這也是一般在台灣，朋友之間會做的事情。幾乎每天你都可以看見人們坐在咖啡廳，聊天、喝飲料。朋友一起在百貨公司裡購物。我們也喜歡聚在朋友的家裡。我們也可能會去餐廳來社交，同時填飽他們的肚子。對於有特殊共同的嗜好和興趣的朋友，他們可能會組織像是樂團練習、保齡球賽、讀書會等等活動。你也可以看見青少年在閒逛或是無目的消磨時光，或者在麥當勞，那裡的食物跟飲料是付得起的，而且他們的地方可以讓你坐一整

a place where it is possible to spend all day.

天。

In addition, there are many places in Taiwan which are sleepless, or open 24 hours a day. To summarize, no matter what we do, keeping each other company regularly is important to maintain friendships.

此外，在台灣有很多地方是不夜城，24小時開放。總之，不論我們做什麼，定期陪伴彼此，對於維持友誼很重要的。

關鍵單字解密

1. socialize *v.* 社交	2. wander *v.* 閒逛
3. hang out *v. slang* 消磨時光	4.. aimlessly *adj.* 無目的的

文法應用解析、深入應用補一補

❶ For friends who have special shared hobbies... study groups, and so on.

解析

For friends who/whom... 也是關係子句的例子，主格用 who，**受格**用 whom。"For people who…" **就是 "凡是怎麼樣的人"。**

其它應用

For friends whom you have chemistry with, you can enjoy each other's company, no matter what you do or where you go.（對凡是和你有化學作用的朋友，無論你們做什麼或去哪裡都可以享受彼此的陪伴。）

❷ Keeping each other company regularly is important to maintain friendships.

解析

Ving is adj/N.是動名詞當主詞的句型，一個動名詞當主詞，用單數的動詞，後面接形容詞或是名詞作補語。

其它應用

Keeping in touch with friends is important; however, spending time with your family is very important, too.（和朋友保持聯絡是很重要的；然而，和你的家人共度時光也是非常重要的。）

5-3 談網路交友

|應用句型|
動詞、名詞詞性轉換

|搭配口說主題|
談網路交友

重點文法搶先看

① 各種詞性轉換

重要句型與文法放大鏡

本單元繼續談「詞性轉換」。把動詞轉換名詞用，是比較學術的寫作用法，而且也會讓人有耳目一新的感覺；下表列出一些例子：

動詞	名詞
appoint 指定、委任	appointment
assign 指定、派用	assignment
discuss 討論	discussion
use 使用	for the use of
search 搜尋	in search of
pursue 購買	in pursue of

更多本單元主題一些例子：

① **accept—acceptance 接受**

例 If you accept all Facebook friend requests that come your way, this acceptance may make you vulnerable.（如果你接受所有臉書朋友的請求，那麼這個接受可能讓你受傷害。）

② **select—selection 選擇**

例 Always be more selective about whom you approve to be your friends on social media; this selection can prevent you from possible frauds.（永遠要好好選擇在社交媒體上的朋友，選得好能讓你避免可能的詐騙活動。）*可以用形容詞換句話說：selective 選擇性的，例：So, always be selective.（所以總是要有選擇性。）

③ **caution—caution 警告**

例 1 The newspaper warned social media users about reading and posting everything on social media.（報紙警告社交媒體的使用者，在社交媒體上閱讀和公告每件事情時都要小心。）*注意：在這裡不用 caution 這個動詞，因為 warn 這個動詞更搭配此情形。例 2 Therefore, you should read and post everything on social media with caution.（因此，對於社群媒體上，每件事的解讀和公告，你都該非常謹慎。）*注意：而這裡是慣用 caution；而非 warning。

文法和口說應用大結合

以上文法和句型可以運用到 IBT、NEW TOEIC 及 IELTS 考試上面，以下列的題目舉例 Track 21

Social media are web-based communication tools that enable people to interact with each other by both sharing and consuming information. Do you make friends through social media? Do you think it is a useful tool or something you need to be concerned about?

社交媒體是以網路進行的溝通工具，它使人們可以藉由分享和消費資訊互相交流。你會經由社交媒體交朋友嗎？你認為它是一個有用的工具，或是必須要擔心的事情呢？

高分範文

I am a frequent user of Facebook. I like it because it is a very useful tool to understand what my friends currently do; at the same time, it is very convenient for me to post my news, so every friend on the site can know what is happening to

我是經常使用臉書的人。我喜歡它，因為它是非常有用的工具，讓我知道我的朋友現在在做什麼；對我來說也非常方便，我可以張貼我的新消息，所以每個網站上的朋友，都可以

me without any effort on my part to contact them individually.

知道我現在發生什麼事情，而不用我一一通知他們。

It reminds you of your friends' birthdays, You can have conversations with friends on the site for free if you are connected to the Internet. However, I know people who are concerned about online privacy and safety. Well, it is not my concern because I know how to protect myself.

它提醒你你的朋友的生日。只要你連結到網路，你可以和朋友在網站上免費對話。然而，我知道一些人會擔心網路隱私和安全。我不擔心這些，因為我知道怎麼保護自己。

I know you cannot trust everyone who requests you to be Facebook friends. For me, I refuse to befriend total strangers; I will only consider people who have mutual friends with me. I choose and categorize friends. Some friends can only see my profile pictures and name. What

我知道你不能相信在臉書上每個要求和你做朋友的人。對我而言，我拒絕和完全的陌生人交朋友。我只考慮和我有共同朋友的人做朋友。我選擇朋友並將朋友做分類，一些朋友只能看到我的頭像照片

that means is that my life on Facebook is specifically for those who are close to me. To summarize, I filter friends, choose who can see my news and pictures to protect myself and also allow my real friends to keep each other updated.

和名字。這表示我在臉書上的生活，只特別讓和我親近的人分享。結論是，我過濾朋友、選擇誰可以看到我的動態和照片，以保護我自己，也允許我真正的朋友彼此更新現況。

關鍵單字解密

1. privacy *n.* 隱私	2. befriend *v.* 做朋友
3. mutual *adj.* 共同的	4. profile *n.* 側面（像）；輪廓；外形
5. filter *v.* 過濾	

文法應用解析、深入應用補一補

❶ So every friend on the site can know what is happening to me without... individually.

解析

"with" 是什麼事情必須伴隨什麼的事，才可能發生；例：You

can send me a message with your new smart phone. 而 “without” 是什麼事情不用伴隨什麼的事，即可發生。“without” 與 “not” 連用，形成雙重否定，也就是負負得正。

其它應用

You cannot accept friend requests from everyone without filtering. 你不能接受任何人的交友請求，而不用過濾。 **提點** （也就是說你必須要過濾朋友請求）這是雙重否定（double negative）的例子

❷ It is not my concern because I know how to protect myself.

解析

“concern” 是名詞，表示擔心的事、認為重要的事；“something is not your concern” 表示沒有你的事情，和你無關，你不用擔心。

其它應用

Social media today brings together the news, trends, socializing and digital marketing. However, the safety of social media marketing is one of my concerns.（今日的社交媒體將新聞、趨勢、社交和數位電子市場結合在一起。然而，社交媒體市場的安全性是我所擔心的事情之一。）

5-4 同事友誼

| 應用句型 |
現在簡單式

| 搭配口說主題 |
同事友誼

重點文法搶先看

① 使用現在式的原則

② 現在式代替未來式的情況

重要句型與文法放大鏡

自本單元起，我們介紹口語中常會用的三種時態，即現在式、未來和完成式。時態簡單的來說，就是在句子中表示出時間的狀態。在中文，我們通常只加上時間副詞，譬如昨天、前天、將來。而在英文當中，動詞也必須跟著做變化。基本上的時態有現在、過去、未來、進行，本單元先介紹簡單現在式。

① **現在式是用來表示長時間不會變的習慣、事實、真理及情感，表達論點時，大多數的情況是用現在式。** 例 1 It is necessary to make friends with co-workers, especially when you are a new arrival in the workplace.（和同事做朋友是很必要的，特別當你是工作場所的新人時。）

例 2 Otherwise, you can feel like an unwanted outsider and feel isolated.（否則，你會感覺自己是沒有人要的局外人，也會感覺被孤立。）

例 3 Then the work-place can become a more enjoyable place to go to because you feel included and cared about.（那麼工作場所可以變成一個更舒服的地方，因為你感覺你是其中一員，而且被關心。）

② 句子中有表時間或條件的連接詞（例如：when, before, after, as soon as, if, until），且當主要子句是未來式時，副詞／從屬子句要用現在式代替未來式。

例 There are reasons to keep a distance from your co-workers. If you choose a bad friend, they may just gossip about you and your work life will be much more complicated. A bad friend at work can cause big problems that aren't easily fixed.（有一些和同事保持距離的理由。如果你選擇到了壞朋友，他們可能會八卦你的事情，那麼你的工作生活就會變得更複雜。工作上的壞朋友可能會給你造成不容易解決的大麻煩。）

 文法和口說應用大結合

以上文法和句型可以運用到 IBT、NEW TOEIC 及 IELTS 考試上面，以下列的題目舉例 Track 22

Would you make friends with co-workers? What are the pros and cons of making friends at work?

你會跟同事做朋友嗎？跟工作上的同事做朋友有什麼優點和缺點？

 高分範文

Yes, I make friends with my colleagues. However, I am aware that becoming friends with co-workers can be tricky, so you need to be selective.

是的，我喜歡和我的同事做朋友。然而，我也意識到和同事做朋友可能是很複雜的。所以，你必須要懂得選擇。

On the one hand, having a friend at work can make your working place more comfortable because you know your friends will help you, support you and

一方面，在工作場合上有朋友時，你的工作環境會變得更舒服，因為你知道你的朋友可以幫助你、支持你，並

give you confidence. A friendlier work environment boosts more creativity. You feel more comfortable being yourself and this enables you to think outside the box. Having a friend at work gives you an outlet to release your emotions and frustrations; therefore, you will rebound quicker from those negative feelings.

且給你信心。一個較友善的工作環境會刺激更多的創造力。你會更自在地做你自己，這使得你能夠超越框架思考。工作場合上的朋友給你出口，渲洩你的情緒和沮喪；因此，你會從那些負面的情感當中恢復的更快。

On the other hand, too much chit-chat in your workplace and any distraction from your job can turn you into an unprofessional employee. Also, getting too close with someone at work may get you into trouble. They know a little bit too much about you, including your demons or weaknesses. If you think someone is your friend and it

另外一方面，太多職場上的閒聊，和從工作上分心，會把你變成不專業的員工。而且，和工作上的某人太接近可能會有麻煩。他們知道一些過多關於你的事情，包括你的心魔和弱點。如果你認為某人是你的朋友，結果到頭來發現不是這一回事，你

turns out not to be the case, you could be backstabbed by someone you trusted. For this reason, you should always remember to keep things professional at all times. Work comes first! It's nice to have support from your friends, but avoid playing favorites.

可能被你認識的人從背後捅了一刀。基於這個理由，應該要永遠記得保持你的專業。工作優先！有朋友的支持雖然很好，但是要避免厚此薄彼。

關鍵單字解密

1. tricky *adj.* 難處理的；微妙的	2. think outside the box *ph.* 打破常規；創新思考
3. unprofessional *adj.* 不專業	4. backstab *v.* 出賣他人；以卑鄙的手段陷害

文法應用解析、深入應用補一補

❶ I am aware that becoming friends with co-workers can be tricky.

解析

aware（知道的；意識到）是形容詞，後面要接 of＋N. 或是 that 子句。

其它應用

I am aware that there are several things you need to notice when you make friends with your colleagues.（我意識到有一些當你和你的同事交朋友的時候，必須注意的事情。）

② **It's nice to have support from your friends, but avoid playing favorites.**

解析

必須接動名詞為受詞的動詞有：avoid 避免；keep、maintain 維持；try 嘗試；enjoy 喜愛；practice 練習；spend 花錢；finish 完成；give up 放棄；waste 浪費；quit 停止……等等。**提點** try to V 是「設法」的意思。

其它應用

Friends can significantly influence how you feel, think and behave. Therefore, you should try maintaining healthy friendships with your colleagues.（朋友可以對你的感覺、思考跟行為上面有很大的影響。因此，你應該嘗試和你的同事維持健康的友誼。）

5-5 同事溝通

| 應用句型 |
未來式

| 搭配口說主題 |
同事溝通

重點文法搶先看

① Will——預測未來時常用 will。

② Be going to——表計畫、意向或行動時。

③ Be about to——表示最近將發生的動作。

④ Be to V 表示計劃或安排好的動作。

重要句型與文法放大鏡

簡單未來式用以表示未來可能發生的事／動作或出現的狀態，或對未來想要做的事。它有兩種句型：shall/will＋原形動詞，或 Be 動詞（am/is/are）＋going to＋原形動詞構成。但兩者有些微的不同，請參見以下介紹。

① Will——預測未來時常用 will

例 1 It is true that you will bond quickly with people that

you have shared interests with.（的確，你將會很地的和你有共同興趣的人結朋友。）例 2 If you follow these basic rules, your co-workers will like you.（如果你遵守這些基本的規則，你的同事將會喜歡你。例 3 Communication and productivity will help you socialize well with your co-workers.（溝通和生產力將會幫助你和你的同事交際得很好。）

② Be going to 表計畫、意向或行動時

例 1 It is very important to keep your salary details to yourself; otherwise, you are going to be fired according to the company's rules.（你必須將你的薪水細節保密這是很重要的，否則根據公司的規則，你將會被開除。）

例 2 If you say you are going to have a project done by a certain time, make sure you adhere to the deadlines.（如果你說你預計在一個特定的時間前要完成一個項目計劃，就必須確保你能夠謹守著那個最後期限日期。）*計劃做什麼事、應該做什麼事、註定要做什麼事。不一定要用"will"或 "be going to"，可用 "be about to" 和 "be to V"。

③ Be about to 表示最近將發生的動作。

例 可將上一句換成：If you say you are about to have a project....

④ Be to V 表示計劃或安排好的動作。

例 The meeting is to be held next Monday morning.

文法和口說應用大結合

以上文法和句型可以運用到 IBT、NEW TOEIC 及 IELTS 考試上面，以下列的題目舉例 Track 23

What do you think the basic rules are when you work with your colleagues?

你認為跟同事一起工作的時候，有哪些基本準則呢？

高分範文

Yes, it is true that there are definitely some rules to keep in mind in the workplace. The first rule is that you should not divulge certain information to your co-workers, but keep it to yourself, for example, salary, financial history and details of your job reviews. On the other

是的，的確在工作場所有一些準則要牢記在心的。第一個準則是你不應該洩露特定的資訊給你的同事，例如薪水、財務史與工作表現評論報告的細節或者是在另一方面，你必須要誠實；對你在工作場所

hand, you need to be honest; be honest about your **capabilities** in the workplace, the real you, your strengths and your weaknesses. You should make an effort to **portray** and maximize your skills honestly.

上的能力誠實；讓你的同事看見真實的你，你的強項和你的弱點。你應該要盡力描繪以及誠實的發揮你最大的技能。

Also, don't pretend to be someone else, just be yourself. You do not have to agree with everything that your co-workers say; in fact, different opinions can lead to healthy conversations and debates. Furthermore, be **trustworthy**. You need to do your best to meet your deadlines to win their trust. In addition, be a team player. If you can prove your willingness to work hard, and be productive, co-workers will appreciate you as an asset to team goals and

還有，不要假裝自己當別人，就當你自己就好。你不必同意同事所說的每一件事；事實上，不同的意見可以引發健康的對話和辯論。再者，要值得信賴。你需要盡你所能地滿足你的截止時間，以贏得他們的信任。此外，要有團隊合作精神。如果你可以證明你對努力工作的意願，以及你的生產力，同事們會欣賞你，將你視為團隊目標的資

want to get to know you on a more personal level.

產，然後就會想要認識更多你個人的層面的事情。

Last but not least, be humorous. Everyone appreciates humor in friendships, but be careful not to offend anyone. We should keep these points in mind to achieve an enjoyable workplace.

最後一點但不是最不重要的，要有幽默感。每個人都欣賞友誼中的幽默，但是要小心，不要冒犯任何人。我們應該把這一些要點牢記在心裡，成就一個愉快的工作場所。

關鍵單字解密

1. divulge *v.* 洩露	2. capability *n.* 能力
3. portray *v.* 描繪	4. trustworthy *adj.* 值得信賴

文法應用解析、深入應用補一補

❶ You need to do your best to meet your deadlines to win their trust.

解析

do your best 字面上是「做你的最好的」，既然要做你最好的，就是表示盡你的全力，好好的去做！盡你最大的能力！

其它應用

You should do your best to be a team-player. This means you can build workplace relationships and socialize normally.（你必須盡你最大的能力成為團隊的一員。這意味著你能建立職場上的關係，並且正常的交際。）

❷ We should keep these points in mind to enable an enjoyable workplace.

解析

keep something in mind-把什麼事情記在心上，就是牢記於心的意思。也可以使用：These/there are some things to keep in mind（**這些／有一些事情必須牢記於心**）。

其它應用

There are some things to keep in mind in the workplace: be a team-player, be approachable and be open to ideas.（有一些在工作場所的事情必須牢記於心：要成為團隊的一員、要隨時可以找得到人，並且對不同的意見持開放的態度。）

5-6 科技媒體與社交

｜應用句型｜
as I have said 就像我說的……

｜搭配口說主題｜
科技媒體與社交

重點文法搶先看

① As I have said...

② 肯定句句型 S+has/have+(adv.)+Vpp.；否定句句型 S+has/have+not (never)+Vpp.+(adv.)。

③ 被動語氣（Passive）肯定句的句型：S+has/have+been+Vp.p.

④ Having said... 是 as I have said... 的分詞構句

重要句型與文法放大鏡

“As I have said” 字面上是：如同我已經說過的，常常可以譯為：就我之前所說的，是現在完成式的句子，現在我們先來解析現在完成式。**現在完成式表過去的某個動作，到現在已經完成，或是某個動作從過去的持續到現在。現在完成式的動詞要用過去分詞來展現。詳細用法如下：**

① **肯定句的句型：S＋has/have＋(adv.)＋Vpp.** 提點 第三人稱單數的主詞用 has，其他用 have。否定句的句型：**S＋has/have＋not (never)＋Vpp.＋(adv.).** 注意：has not = hasn't、have not = haven't

例 With the rise of social media, it has become easier to develop new friendships.（社交媒體的崛起，使得發展新的友誼變得更容易。）

② **被動語氣（Passive）肯定句的句型：S＋has/have＋been＋Vp.p.**

例 As smartphones have been used for these ten years or more, people have slowly reduced face-to-face meetings.（當智慧型手機已經被使用超過十年，人們也變得緩慢地減少見面。）

③ **Having said... 是 as I have said... 的分詞構句**

例 Having said their disadvantages, I cannot deny the convenience web-based communication tools bring to life. For example, they allow you to send instant messages, document or picture files.（我已經談過他們的缺點，但不能否認網路溝通工具對生活帶來的便利。例如，它們可以允許你傳送立即的訊息文件或是圖片檔案。）

提點 也可以解為 Although（雖然）這個連接詞被省略了。

文法和口說應用大結合

以上文法和句型可以運用到 IBT、NEW TOEIC 及 IELTS 考試上面，以下列的題目舉例 Track 24

Mobile phone-based and web-based communication tools appear to play a significant role in people's daily lives. However, some people argue that social media has replaced face-to-face interaction with people. What is your opinion on this?

手機和網路為基礎的溝通工具顯然在人們的日常生活中扮演重要的角色。然而，一些人爭論說社交媒體已經取代了人們面對面的交流。你的想法是什麼呢？

高分範文

Yes, indeed, the technology in developing mobile phone-based and web-based communication tools has been greatly enhanced. In the old days, we needed to send messages by post, which took time and postage to be delivered.

是的，的確，在發展手機和網路為基礎的溝通工具的科技已經進步很多。過去，我們需要郵寄訊息，信件都要花時間和郵資才能被送達。國際電話非常貴。然而，現在只要你能夠

International calls were still very costly. However, nowadays, you can send messages, pictures or files for free, as long as you are connected to the Internet. The fee for the Internet is much more affordable.

上網，你就可以免費傳送訊息、圖片或是檔案。連網的費用更能付得起。

Additionally, with the rise of social media, such as Facebook and mobile phone Apps, you can find friends who you haven't been in touch with for a long time. Without these inventions, it's easy to lose touch with old friends.

此外，社交媒體的崛起，像是臉書和手機的 APP 使你可以找到你很久沒有聯絡的朋友。沒有這些發明，很容易和老朋友失去聯絡的。

Having stated their advantages, they also come with negative impacts. Many people unduly rely on these virtual tools and neglect real time being with friends and family. As has been

談了它們的優點後，它們也伴隨者負面的影響。很多人過度依賴這些虛擬的工具，然後忽略和他們朋友、家人真正相處的時間。如

seen, these tools certainly have changed the way people interact.

我們所見，這些工具確實已經改變人類交流方式。

As I have said, the inventions of these communication tools are brilliant; however, we should be aware that we should never let these technology tools replace the need for face-to-face interactions.

如之前所說，這些溝通工具的發明真是很傑出；然而，我們應該要意識到我們不應該讓傳送簡訊，或是社交媒體，取代面對面交流的需要。

關鍵單字解密

1. postage *n.* 郵資	2. affordable *adj.* 付得起
3. unduly *adv.* 過度地	4. brilliant *adj.* 絕妙的

文法應用解析、深入應用補一補

❶ With the rise of social media, such as Facebook and mobile phone Apps, you can find friends who you haven't been in touch with for a long time

解析

“The rise of something” 是「……的出現、崛起」；“with the rise of something” 是有著、以、隨著……的出現、崛起

其它應用

With the rise of smartphones, a variety of Apps have been invented accordingly.（隨著智慧型手機的崛起，很多的 APP 也已隨之被發明。）

❷ As has been seen, these tools certainly have changed the way people interact.

解析

“As has been seen,”（已經可以看出），和 “As can be seen”（可以看出），都是 As = which 代表之前的完整句子，例：These tools certainly have changed the way people interact, which has been seen.“ Which” 被 “as” 取代，放在句首。

其它應用

As has been seen, these tools may discourage real time with friends or family.（已經可以看到的是，這些工具可能會阻止和朋友、家人實際的相處時間。）

6-1 環保與經濟發展

｜應用句型｜
Let's think about what will happen... 我們來看看會發生什麼事……

｜搭配口說主題｜
環保與經濟發展

重點文法搶先看

① wh——之名詞子句

② 有「是否」的意思用 "whether" or "if"

重要句型與文法放大鏡

名詞子句是一種附屬子句，亦即必須依附主要子句才能存在。名詞子句做名詞用，即主要做主詞或受詞。名詞子句和名詞的差別是：名詞子句多了一個主詞和動詞，有主詞和動詞就形成了子句。有子句就要有連接詞來和主要子句連接。連接詞包括：what（見 Ch6 6-2）、that（見 Ch6 6-3），以及其他的疑問詞，例如：when、where，則將在這一單元介紹。

① wh——之名詞子句

試著想：**並不是許多人都考慮過它對環境產生了多少的成本** 這一句怎麼說；由於它都有第二個主詞（許多人、它）、動詞（考慮和產生）和疑問詞（多少），所以就需要連接詞，而此疑問詞本身就可作連接詞。

整句先翻 **它對環境產生了多少的成本**。→框起的句子先用 it 代替：Not many people think about it. 也就是：主詞＋及物動詞＋受詞之基本句型的句子；it= how much does it cost to the environment? 最後兩句合併起來，不倒裝，也就是去掉助動詞，最後成為：Not all people think about [how much it costs to the environment]. 這裡將名詞子句標示在中括弧 [ ] 裡面。

② 有是否的意思用 “whether” or “if”

試著想：很少人會想到 **這些活動是否會帶來相對應的成本到環境中** 怎麼說，整句拆解、合併過程如下：

→ Few people think of it.

→ it = if/ whether they bring accordingly related costs to the environment or not

→ Few people think of [whether they bring costs to the environment].

文法和口說應用大結合

以上文法和句型可以運用到 IBT、NEW TOEIC 及 IELTS 考試上面，以下列的題目舉例 Track 25

There have been keen debates about the relationship between economic development and environmental protection. What are your views? Explain your ideas.

一直有關於經濟發展和環境保護兩者之間關係的熱烈討論。你的觀點是什麼？請解釋你的想法。

高分範文

There are unavoidable conflicts between economic development and environmental protection. Economic activities, in both production and consumption, are related to the environment in two fundamental ways - we draw resources from the environment to produce goods and services, and we emit wastes into the environment

經濟發展和環境保護之間有不可避免的衝突。經濟活動同時在生產和消費方面都以兩個基本的方式和環境相關— 我們從天然環境中索取天然資源生產財務和勞務，然後同時在生產和消費的過程當中，我們排放廢棄物。這些損害已經造成了包含土壤

in the process of both producing and consuming. The damage that has been caused includes eroding farmlands, greenhouse gases and acid rain.

酸化、產生溫室氣體和酸雨。

If we really cut down on those economic activities to protect the environment, this will bring a major impact: reducing both individual incomes and the national economy. Therefore, some people strongly oppose this idea. On the other hand, protecting or saving the environment means spending money. However, I would rather consider it as an investment than consumption. We need to do this for those people who live three or four or five generations afterwards.

如果我們減少了這些經濟活動以保護環境，這將會帶來一個重大的影響：同時減少個人的所得，並削弱國家的經濟。因此，一些人強力的反對這個想法。在另一方面，保護和拯救環境意味著花錢，然而，我寧願認為它是一項投資，而非消費。我們必須為了三、四或五個世代以後的人們這麼做。

In short, these human economic activities have consistently been accompanied by an acceleration of ecological degradation, particularly biodiversity loss, pollution and environment crises.

簡而言之，這些人類經濟活動已經持續著伴隨生態惡化的加速，特別是在生物多樣性的損失污染，和環境危機方面。

關鍵單字解密

1. unavoidable *adj.* 不可避免的	2. fundamental *adj.* 基本的
3. investment *n.* 投資	4. consistently *adv.* 持續著地
5. accompany *v.* 伴隨	6. biodiversity *n.* 生物多樣性

文法應用解析、深入應用補一補

❶ Economic activities, in both production and consumption, are related to the environment.

解析

relate 動詞的意思是「把……聯繫起來」；而用形容詞的用法是：A be related to B，表示「A 和 B 有關」。

其它應用

Economic development of a nation often focuses on efficiency. When economists think of efficiency, their consideration is usually related only to the efficiency of labor and capital. They should consider the environment as well.（一個國家的經濟發展通常著眼於效率。經濟學者想到的效率通常只考慮和勞工和資本有關的效率。他們也應該要考慮環境。）

❷ I would rather consider it as an investment than consumption.

解析

“would rather” 意思是「寧願」，表示主觀願望；若是表示兩者之中選擇其一，可加上 “than”，形成 “would rather A than B” 句子，意思是「寧願 A 而不願 B」。

其它應用

Reducing eco-unfriendly economic activities can enhance our quality of life, but it does not contribute to our GNP. I would rather reduce our GNP than continuously harm our earth.（減少對生態不友善的經濟活動可以提升我們生活的品質，但是這對我們的國民生產總值（GNP）沒有幫助。我寧願減少我們的國民生產總值而不是持續地傷害我們的地球。）

6-2 工作輕鬆與挑戰性的抉擇

應用句型	搭配口說主題
The important thing is that... 重要的是……	工作輕鬆與挑戰性的抉擇

重點文法搶先看

① 疑問詞、名詞子句和 that

② 和意見、想法、建議和報告的動詞連用的 that

③ The important/tricky thing/part is that …

④ It is very likely that…/It is possible that…

重要句型與文法放大鏡

① **沒有疑問詞的名詞子句就用 that；② 有關意見、想法、建議和報告的動詞經常使用 that 子句，如：**

例 1 I believe [that the choice depends on what type of person you are and what your goals are.]（我相信這個決定取決於你是哪一類型的人，以及你的目標是什麼。）

提點 that 後到句尾為名詞子句，當 believe 的受詞。

例 2 I agree [that when choosing a job, you might consider what you're good at and what you're passionate about.]*（我同意找工作的時候，你可能考慮你擅長什麼，以及對於什麼有熱情。）提點 that 後到句尾為名詞子句，當 agree 的受詞。

③ **常用句：The important/tricky thing/part is that... 重要／棘手的事情／部分是……**

例 The important thing is that you need to know your goals when choosing a job.（重要的事情是當你選擇工作時，需要知道你的目標。）

④ **這句話也很實用：It is very likely that…/It is possible that… 很有可能……**

例 It is possible **that** an easy job can become very hard when you start to lose the motivation to work.（這有可能發生的，當你在開始失去動力，一個輕鬆的工作可能會變得非常難。）

文法和口說應用大結合

以上文法和句型可以運用到 IBT、NEW TOEIC 及 IELTS 考試上面，以下列的題目舉例 Track 26

Which do you prefer: to have a challenging job, or to have an easy job where you don't have to work hard?
你的偏好是下列哪一種：有挑戰性的工作，或是不必努力、輕鬆的工作？

高分範文

To have a challenging job or not to have a challenging job? That is the question. It really depends on a range of factors, which include: the type of person you are, what your goals are and the life stage you are at.

要有輕鬆的工作，還是不要？那是個問題。這問題實在是取決於很多的因素，這些因素包含：你是哪一種類型的人、你的目標是什麼、還有你的人生是在哪一個階段。

In terms of personality, I am the kind of person who wants to work hard. Regarding life goals,

以個性而言，我是想要努力工作的類型。以人生目標而言，就我

as far as I am concerned, leading an easy life is not my life goal. Personal development is always my priority. I find having a challenging job motivates me to work harder. I can gain more from challenging jobs and the experience can provide me with new perspectives and broaden my horizons.

個人而言，過著輕鬆的人生不是我的人生目標。個人的發展一直是我的優先考量。我發現挑戰性的工作給我動力去作。我可以從挑戰性的工作中，學到很多，並且這個經驗可以提供我新的看法和擴展我的視野。

I am talking from a personal growth perspective; however, things may change when I have children. I may focus more on my family. Most importantly, no matter what your preference is, at least devote your time and energy to work during working hours.

我現在是從個人發展的角度來說；然而，當我有孩子的時候，事情可能就不同了。我可能會更重視我的家庭。最重要的是，不論你的偏好是什麼，至少你在工作時間能夠致力你的時間和精力在工作上。

關鍵單字解密

1. challenging *adj.* 具挑戰性的	2. priority *n.* 優先
3. broaden *v.* 擴展	4. horizon *n.* 視野
5. devote to *v.* 致力於	

文法應用解析、深入應用補一補

❶ I am the kind of person who wants to work hard.

解析

表示你是哪一種人的說法："I am the kind of person who+v... "，形容詞子句的用法（見 Ch6 6-4、6-5）。

其它應用 1

I am the kind of person who values family and friends more than work.（我是那一種重視家庭和朋友多於工作的人。）

其它應用 2

I am the kind of person who is very engaged in work and likes challenges.（我是那一種非常投入於工作和喜歡挑戰的人。）

❷ I am talking from a personal growth perspective.

解析

「從……角度來看」的說法：雖說是「看」，英文用的還是 "talk"（說）："talking from a... perspective"；若 perspective 之前的形容詞太長，可用 of 所有格的方法放在 of 後面→Talking from the perspective of…。

其它應用

Talking from the perspective of work-life balance, when you care more about work-life balance than improving your skills, you can take a job that emphasizes shorter working hours.（從工作——生活平衡的角度來看，當你重視你的工作——生活的平衡多於改進你的技巧，你可以選擇做強調較短工時的工作。）

6-3 學歷之必要性、對學歷之看法

應用句型	搭配口說主題
The reason that comes to mind is that... 我所想到的理由是……	學歷之必要性、對學歷之看法

重點文法搶先看

① The reason that comes to mind is＋that＋子句

② what、that、whether 子句之區別

重要句型與文法放大鏡

① 除了用 “because” 來「給理由」之外，想拿高分的英文說法有：“The reason that comes to mind is＋that＋子句”（我所想到的理由是……），注意在 “reason” 之後是用關代——“that”，而非“why”，這是因為 “reason” 已經包含了 “why” 的意思，所以說 “the reason why” 是重複又多餘的。也要注意我們在 Be 動詞之後用是 “that” 接名詞子句，而非 “because”。

例 Educational certificates are very important. The reason that comes to mind is **that** almost every professional company and international entrepreneurs require candidates to have certain higher educational degrees.（教育文憑非常重要。我所想到的理由是，幾乎每一個專業的公司和國際企業都需要候選人有一定的高等教育程度。）

② **現在來看名詞子句中 what、that、whether 之區別句型**

★ 說出描述一件事：主要子句 ***that*** S +V …（見例 1）

★ 未說出什麼事：主要子句 ***what*** S +V …（見例 2）

★ 不確定之事：主要子句 ***whether/ if*** S +V …（見例 3）名詞子句做主詞時當然放句首，如例 3。

例 1 The reason that comes to mind is [that society teaches me a lot of things which I couldn't learn at school].（我所想到的理由是，這個社會教給我許多學校沒有教我的事情。）

例 2 Some university students have no idea of [what they should do in the university].（一些大學生根本不知道他們在大學裡應該做什麼。）

例 3 [Whether a university degree is necessary] depends on what you want to do for your career.（大學文憑是否是必要的，取決於你想做什麼職業。）**提點** that 常常可以省略，但是不能省略的情況有：（1）句首 That 不可省（2）that 直接碰上 be 動詞，如這兩頁在例句中提到的 that。

文法和口說應用大結合

以上文法和句型可以運用到 IBT、NEW TOEIC 及 IELTS 考試上面，以下列的題目舉例 Track 27

Do you agree or disagree with the following statement? A university education is necessary for success in today's world. Explain your reasons in detail.

你同意或是不同意以下的陳述：想要在現在的社會中成功，大學教育是非常重要的。請仔細解釋你的理由。

高分範文

I partly agree with this statement. To have a university certificate is very important in this society; however, it does not mean a ticket to success. Having a higher education is essential. The reason that comes to mind is that many job positions are only open to people who have a certain higher education degree. In those cases, without a degree,

我部分同意這個陳述。在這個社會當中，有大學文憑是非常重要的；然而，它並不保證是通往成功的車票。有較高的教育是必要的。我能想到的理由是，很多工作職位只開放給有一定高學歷的人。在那些情況之下，沒有文憑，要找一個好的以及

finding a good and well-paid job is tough. The second reason is that a university can be a temple of knowledge if students go there to learn. Universities are supposed to hire knowledgeable and enthusiastic teachers, to provide learning resources for students to reference on their own and with cutting-edge devices. That way, students can learn required knowledge and important skills for them to apply in their future jobs.

待遇高的工作是很困難的。第二個理由是，如果學生是去學習，大學是知識的殿堂，大學應該僱用有知識、有熱誠的老師，也提供學習資源給學生當自學的參考，以及提供最尖端的設備。這麼一來，學生就可以學習必要的知識和重要的技能，應用在將來的工作上面。

Moreover, university is often the place where a student can meet and become friends with teaching staff and other students. The relationships or even friendships can help to further careers.

更甚者，大學經常是一個學生們見面以及和教職員和其他學生交朋友的地方。這個關係或是甚至友誼可以幫助他們未來的職業。

Having said that, the benefits of having a university degree are not applicable to everyone, for example, those who aim to become salespersons, plumbers or carpenters. People in such careers can also be successful, and make more money than a university graduate.

話雖如此，大學文憑的好處並不適用於每一個人，例如，那些目標定在成為推銷員、水電工或是木匠的人。那些職位的人們也可以很成功，並且賺得比大學畢業生還要多的錢。

關鍵單字解密

1. certificate *n.* 證書、文憑	2. temple *n.* 寺廟、殿堂
3. cutting-edge *adj.* 尖端的	4. applicable *adj.* 可適用的

文法應用解析、深入應用補一補

❶ Universities are supposed to hire knowledgeable and enthusiastic teachers, to provide....

解析

"be supposed to..." 其中 to 是動詞不定詞，不是介系詞，其後要跟動詞原形。當 be supposed to... 的主詞是"人"時，意「應該⋯⋯」；「被期望⋯⋯」，它可以用來表示勸告、建議、義務、責任等，不相當於情態動詞——"should"；"be supposed to" 是基於法律、規則或習俗，應該⋯⋯，而 "should"是勸告、建議的意思而已。

其它應用

University students **are supposed to** invest their time and money in acquiring knowledge and skills from their universities.（大學生應該投資他們的時間和金錢，以從大學獲得知識和技巧。）

❷ **Having said that**, the benefits of having a university degree are not applicable to everyone.

解析

"Having said that," 是 "Although/though I have said that⋯"完成式分詞構句的形式，詳見於 Chapter 7 介紹。

其它應用

University certificates are often the criterion in job recruitment. **Having said that**, work experience is also a requirement which employers look at.（大學文憑通常是工作招聘的必要條件。話雖如此，工作經驗也是雇主們所看中的必要條件。）

6-4 環保與觀光

｜應用句型｜
前位修飾與後位修飾

｜搭配口說主題｜
環保與觀光

重點文法搶先看

① 前位修飾：（中文）形容詞／片語／子句＋名詞

② 後位修飾：形容詞子句

重要句型與文法放大鏡

關係代名詞子句（relative clauses），又稱形容詞子句，由來可從形容詞之作用（即修飾名詞）説起。中文多是前位修飾，即形容詞放名詞前面。

① **前位修飾：（中文）形容詞／片語／子句＋**名詞；**英文形容詞只有一個字時，是用前位修飾，**例 1：He is a selfish tourist. 否則放名詞後面，即後位修飾：名詞＋形容詞／片語／子句。

② 後位修飾，例 2 自私和只顧自己的觀光客通常會亂丟垃圾。→Tourists often litter.「自私和只顧自己的」是觀光客的形容詞，用後位修飾→Tourists [who are selfish and care about themselves] often litter.

這句就是含有關係代名詞子句，或形容詞子句的句子放 [ ] 內；注意到上個例句出現了 who 嗎？這個 Who 即**是關係代名詞**。**當**句中出現第二個動詞（are）時就需要**連接詞**（who）。**關係子句中的連接詞，兼具連接詞及代名詞的功能，稱為關係代名詞，簡稱關代。**關係代名詞子句放要到被修飾名詞（即稱先行詞）的後面，把握**後位修飾的原則即是造句原則。**先看下表**關係代名詞的種類：**

環保與觀光	關代主格+V	受格+S+V
代替**人**	who	whom
代替**物**（東西、動物）	which	which
代替**人／物**	that	that

例 2 Some popular trails, such as in Nepal, have become known as the "Coca-Cola trail" and "Toilet paper trail".（一些如在尼泊爾的有名小徑，已成為大家所知的 "可口可樂足跡" 和 "衛生紙小道"。）

文法和口說應用大結合

以上文法和句型可以運用到 IBT、NEW TOEIC 及 IELTS 考試上面，以下列的題目舉例 Track 28

What is the impact of tourism on the environment?
觀光對於環境有哪些影響呢？

高分範文

Tourism brings money to the local and national economy, but it also has adverse environmental effects. It has put a strain on natural resources which are already scarce because developing tourism needs to construct general infrastructure such as tourism facilities, roads and airports. This can lead to natural habitat loss and increased pressure on endangered species.

觀光業為地方帶來了金錢和帶動國家經濟，但仍對環境帶來負面的影響。由於觀光需要建設，如道路及機場等，這已對稀少的天然資源增加了壓力。這對導至自然棲息地的消失，即將絕跡的物種也會感受壓力。

Also, tourism transportation can cause many forms of pollution; for example, **releasing** CO2 emissions consequently results in acid rain, global warming and photochemical pollution.

同時，觀光業的交通往來也會帶來各種形式的汙染，例如二氧化碳的**釋放**會帶來酸雨、全球暖化和光害汙染。

On the other hand, tourism can serve as a tool to finance protection and **conservation** of natural areas or historic sites with its economic sources. However, considering its adverse aspects, there is a lot to think about in terms of environmental values and economic importance.

另一方面，觀光業也能提供金援，**保育**自然地區或古蹟。但是考量到其負面影響，關於環境價值和經濟重要性上，我們仍有諸多需要考量。

關鍵單字解密

1. adverse *adj.* 不利的	2. strain *n.* 勞損
3. scarce *n.* 稀少	4. infrastructure *n.* 基礎設施
5. release *n.* 釋放	6. conservation *n.* 保育

文法應用解析、深入應用補一補

❶ It has put a strain on natural resources which are already scarce.

解析

"put a strain/pressure on 某人／某事"（加壓力於某人／某事上面）

其它應用

Tourism has put pressure on deforestation by collecting fuel and furnishing wood, as well as developing infrastructures.（旅遊業已因為收集燃料和家具的木材，以及發展基礎建設，對於森林砍伐造成壓力。）

❷ ... considering its adverse aspects, there is a lot to think about in terms of environmental values and economic importance.

解析

"Considering"是"if we consider….."的分詞構句；consider +ving 或名詞子句

其它應用

Considering tourism's negative impact on ecology, the number of tourists should be controlled.（考慮觀光業在生態上的負面影響，觀光客的數量應該被控制。）

6-5 國際村、國際聯盟之看法

| 應用句型 |
of which 關係代名詞用法

| 搭配口說主題 |
國際村、國際聯盟

重點文法搶先看

① 關係代名詞所有格

② 形容詞子句之限定及補述用法

重要句型與文法放大鏡

① 關係代名詞所有格

先行詞	關代主格＋V	受格＋S＋V	所有格＋N＋V
代替**人**	who	whom	whose
代替**物**（東西、動物）	which	which	of which
代替人及物	that	that	of which

上個單元我們介紹了**關係代名詞的主格**和**受格**，本單元我們增加所有格代名詞的用法。先看下表**關係代名詞種類：**

例 1 I appreciate an idea that countries form a single market in **which** goods, people, and capital can move freely.（我欣賞國家之間形成一個單一市場的想法，在那裡

物品、人們和資本都可以自由的流動。）提點 此例是**受格**的用法。

例 2 Some nations of which economy is better need to help nations which have financial problems.（一些經濟好的國家，需要幫助財務有困難的國家。）提點 此例是**所有格**的用法。

② **形容詞子句之限定及補述用法**

★ **限定用法**：先行詞如 the man、people 在世界上都**不只一個**，所以用關代子句把它限定起來，才知道你在講那一個。例：Twenty-two EU members participate in the Schengen area of free movement which allows individuals to travel without passport checks among most European countries.（22 個歐盟會員參加申根地區的自由移動，允許個人在大部分的歐洲國家旅遊不用被檢查護照。）提點 **不只一個** movement

★ **補述用法**：關代之前加逗號是補述用法，指唯一的一個，補充說明先行詞的情況。例：The European Union (EU), which/that is a political and economic partnership, represents a unique form of cooperation among the 28 member states.（歐盟是一個政治和經濟的合夥關係，在 28 個會員國家之間，呈現了一個獨特形式的合作。）

提點 **只有一個** EU

文法和口說應用大結合

以上文法和句型可以運用到 IBT、NEW TOEIC 及 IELTS 考試上面，以下列的題目舉例 Track 29

How do you like the idea of global villages where countries form a league and their citizens can move freely without visas and also work across these countries? 你對地球村的概念有什麼看法？即國家形成一個聯盟，他們的市民可以自由的移動，不需要簽證，也可以在這些國家工作。

高分範文

Yes, I like the idea of nations making up local circles and lives connected to each other like in villages and the neighborhood. The advantages of a union of nations are to promote peace and economic prosperity. If countries can share some sovereignty in economics and trade, it is envisaged that this can reduce the likelihood of wars

是的，我很喜歡國家構成地區圈，生活彼此相連，像是在村莊和鄰里一般。國家結盟的好處是可以提升和平和經濟繁榮。如果國家可以分享在經濟和貿易上的一些主權，可以設想的是，這可以減少戰爭的可能性，因為沒有理由爭鬥，爭鬥的原因通

because there will be no reasons for fighting, which are usually for better lands, resources and markets. Talking from the perspective of the economic benefit, take the European Union or EU for example, they have a unified currency, which is the Euro, and this makes business easier. If people can trade freely across these countries without tariffs, export or import taxes, goods and services must be cheaper.

常是為了要更好的土地、資源和市場。從經濟利益的角度來看，以歐盟也就是 EU 作為例子，他們有統一的貨幣，也就是歐元，使得商業活動更容易。如果人們可以自由地在這些國家之間貿易不需要關稅、出口和進口稅，商品和服務一定會更便宜。

However, free movement among countries invites a lot of controversies. Some nations whose economy is better needed to help nations which have financial problems. This has become a headache for national leaders. Citizens in some countries

然而，在國家之間的自由移動，也引起了爭議。一些經濟比較好的國家，需要幫助有財務困難的國家，這已經成為了這些國家領袖頭痛的問題。一些國家的市民經常抱怨從別的國

often complain that people from other countries compete for jobs with them. It appears that even though there are so many advantages to forming national economic leagues, the public still has a lot to say regarding the negative sides. As far as I am concerned, I think being united promotes cooperation rather than competition.

家來的人和他們競爭工作。即使形成國際經濟聯盟明顯有很多的好處，民眾還是有很多負面的話要說。就我而言，我認為聯盟提倡的是合作，而不是競爭。

關鍵單字解密

1. sovereignty *n.* 主權	2. envisage *v.* 設想

文法應用解析、深入應用補一補

❶ Take the European Union or EU for example, they have... .

解析

「以……作為例子」可用，"Take something for example,"= "Take something as an example," 注意二者用冠詞的情況，for example 不用冠詞，as an example 用

不定冠詞 “an”。

其它應用

In fact, some governmental and non-governmental organizations, academic networks and some multinational agencies have formed a global network and received positive results. Take these for example, it is beneficial in the formation of a Global Village.（事實上，一些政府和非政府的組織、學術網絡和一些多國的代理（商／組織）已經形成了一個全球網絡，並且獲得正面的效果。以這些作為例子，形成國際村是有好處的。）

❷ It appears that even though there are so many advantages to forming national economic leagues,... .

解析

“appear”有兩個意思：1.「出現」（to start to be seen or to be present）；2.「顯然」，句型是：S＋appear (to be)＋adj、S＋appear (to me)＋to v.，以及 S＋appear (to me)＋[(that）子句]

其它應用

For me, nations binding a global cooperative economy appears to connect cultures among those communities.（對於我而言，國家結合全球合作經濟體，顯然是在這些社區結合了文化。）

6-6 人生最重要的是什麼／金錢的價值

｜應用句型｜
觀點邏輯

｜搭配口說主題｜
人生／金錢的價值

重點文法搶先看

① 邏輯問題 1. 因與果不搭

② 邏輯問題 2. 缺少解釋論點

重要句型與文法放大鏡

本單元強調的是邏輯的部分，邏輯是指上下文通不通順，舉出的例證是否符合提出的論點。邏輯是很重要的，因為不論你的英文再好，如果邏輯有問題的話，主考官也是聽不懂的。現在以人生／金錢的價值這個主題為例，強調這個回答在邏輯上面容易出現哪一方面的問題。

① 邏輯問題 1. 因與果不搭

To be a saver or a spender depends on your personality, willpower and control and, most importantly, your philosophy of money.（要成為一個儲蓄的人或花錢的人，取決於你的個性，意志力和控制力，最重要的是，你的金錢哲學。）

提點 你也許會說這取決於你的收入，但不是。人們可以把所有的收入花光，無論他們一個月是賺 100K 或 2K。

② **邏輯問題 2. 缺少解釋論點**

談到個性：Some people just tend to enjoy the moment of life; they take chances to travel, to explore something. They consider less of the future because they focus more on the present. On the other hand, others are more naturally frugal than others, or they more often think of the future and want to have more savings for later life. The factor of personality also mixes with that of the personal philosophy of money. However, savers are not necessary better than spenders.（有些人只傾向於享受生活的當下；他們把握機會去旅遊，去探索東西。他們對未來考慮較少，因為他們更專注於現在。另一方面，其他人天生地比別人更節儉，或者他們更經常地去想未來，並希望對以後的生活儲蓄更多。個性的因素也混合個人的金錢理念。然而，儲蓄的人並不必然比花錢的人更好。）

提點 但只有論點還不夠，接下來你要為這個論點舉出的例證：For example, what if they save 95% of their monthly income, but they don't enjoy their present lives, or their family hate it because they don't have enough or quality holidays.（例如，如果他們儲蓄每月收入的 95%，但他們不喜歡自己目前的生活，或者他們的家人恨節省，因為他們沒有足夠或有品質的假期。）

文法和口說應用大結合

以上文法和句型可以運用到 IBT、NEW TOEIC 及 IELTS 考試上面，以下列的題目舉例 Track 30

What is your philosophy about spending money? Some people tend to enjoy spending money and save little because they think they should enjoy life while they are young. Others save more money for the future. Which kind of a person are you more likely to be?
你花錢的哲學是什麼？一些人傾向於享受花錢，並且儲蓄很少，因為他們認為他們應該趁他們還年輕的時候享受人生。其他人為未來儲蓄較多的錢。你比較傾向於哪一種人呢？

高分範文

To be a saver or a spender, it depends on your personality, willpower and control and, of course, your philosophy about money. For me, I am more a saver. I am naturally frugal. I don't like wasting money on unnecessary things. I cannot help thinking of the days when I am old. I know I need savings to support my retired life. For most of the time, I consciously think about my spending.

當個儲蓄的人或是花錢的人，這取決於你的個性、意志力和控制力，當然，還有你對金錢的哲學。就我而言，我是比較傾向於儲蓄的人。我是天生的節儉。我不喜歡浪費錢在不必要的東西上面。我不由自主地會想到在我年老後，我知道我需要儲蓄以支持我退休後的生活。我大多會刻意地考慮我的花費。

However, sometimes I am an impulsive buyer. I cannot help shopping for clothes which are in big sales. Therefore, I do have moments of being short of money, and then I ask my mother

然而，有時候我是衝動的購買者。我忍不住買打很多折扣的衣服。因此，我會有缺錢的時候，然後向我媽媽討救兵。我對我的預算

to rescue me. I have a self-awareness about my budgeting and spending habits. Nevertheless, I am not interested in book-keeping. I hear many people suggest keeping books to help you control your finances. I don't feel like doing it. I just need to have a rough idea of how much I can spend each month.

和花費習慣有自覺。然而，我對記帳不感興趣。我聽很多人建議記帳，這會幫忙你控制你的財務。我就是不想要做這個。我只需要對於我每個月可以花多少錢一個大概的觀念。

關鍵單字解密

1. philosophy *n.* 哲學	2. willpower *n.* 意志力
3. frugal *adj.* 節儉	4. impulsive *adj.* 衝動的
5. rescue *v.* 拯救	6. finance *n.* 財務
7. rough *adj.* 大概的	

文法應用解析、深入應用補一補

❶ I cannot help thinking of the days when I am old.

解析

“cannot (couldn’t) help＋V-ing”（忍不住）；和 “can't help but＋V” 別搞混了：**忍不住用** “V-ing”；**不得不用** “but V

其它應用

I cannot help putting all my salary in my safety box and locking it away.（我忍不住把我所有的薪水放在我的保險箱，然後把它鎖起來。）

❷ I don’t feel like doing it.

解析

feel like（想要……）。like 是介系詞，故之後要接名詞或動名詞。當接動名詞時，解釋為「想要做……」，相當於 “would like to＋原形動詞”；接名詞時，解釋為「感覺像……」。

其它應用

I don’t feel like spending most of my money each month. I feel like saving as much as I can.（我不想要每個月把大部份的錢都花完。我喜歡盡可能的存錢。）

7-1 運動與健康

｜應用句型｜
Regarding 關於……

｜搭配口說主題｜
運動與健康

重點文法搶先看

① 分詞構句的拆解

② 無人稱獨立分詞構句

重要句型與文法放大鏡

① 分詞構句是副詞子句、對等子句和形容詞子句的簡化，簡化就由長變短，形成步驟如下：

1. 去連接詞（如 because/when/and/who/which）
2. 去副詞／形容詞子句中的主詞，二子句**主詞相同者**，簡化句**稱分詞構句**；二子句**主詞不同者**，簡化句**稱獨立分詞結構**，子句中的**主詞不能刪去**。

例 1 副詞子句 **After I started to spend time outdoors,** I feel myself getting healthier.

→ 分詞構句 **Starting** to spend time outdoors, I feel myself getting healthier.（在我開始花時間在戶外後，我

感覺自己更健康了。）**二子句主詞都是 I，副詞子句的**主詞可以去掉。**

例 2 主動／對等子句 Sports and outdoor activities are beneficial, whether you join a baseball team or a soccer team, **and spend** a few weeks at summer camp, or just engage in free play.

→ 分詞構句 Sports and outdoor activities are beneficial, no matter you join a baseball or soccer team, **spending** a few weeks at summer camp, or just engage in free play.（無論你是參加棒球隊或足球隊，還是在夏令營渡過幾週，或是只是自由活動，運動和戶外活動都是有益的。）

② **無人稱獨立分詞構句：**

當主詞為有共識卻不明確的主詞，如 People、One、We、They、It ……等，雖然與主要子句主詞不同，卻仍然省略從屬子句中的主詞及其連接詞，形成分詞慣用語、分詞轉作連接詞、分詞轉作介系詞：

★ 分詞慣用語有：Generally speaking、Speaking of、Frankly speaking、considering

★ 分詞轉作連接詞有：Supposing that、Providing that、Provided that

★ 分詞轉作介系詞有：Regarding、According to、Considering、Concerning

文法和口說應用大結合

以上兩個句型可以運用到 IBT、NEW TOEIC 及 IELTS 考試上面，以下列的題目舉例 Track 31

Do you think playing sports or outdoor activities are important and why? Explain your reasons, using specific details in your explanation.

你認為做運動或是戶外活動重要嗎？為什麼？用特定的細節來解釋你的理由。

高分範文

Yes, both playing sports and outdoor activities are important. The main reason is that they are beneficial to your health in several ways. To begin with, sports help you keep healthy physically and psychologically. Perhaps the most obvious benefit of participating in sports is physical fitness. Outdoor activities engage large motor

是的，做運動和戶外活動兩者都是很重要的。主要的理由是，它們對你的健康在很多方面都有益處。首先，運動幫助你保持身體上和心理上的健康。也許運動最明顯的益處是身體的健康。從事戶外活動能增加運動機能，對身體的協調性有所幫助。

functions and help with physical coordination. Sporting activities can train your muscles and outdoor activities can do that in a fun way. They can also help you psychologically. Regarding emotional benefits, participating in sports and spending time outdoors helps you to loosen up and let go of stress.

體育的活動可以訓練你的肌肉，而戶外的活動能用有趣的方式來達成這個作用。它們也可以有心理上的幫助。關於情緒上的好處，參加運動和戶外活動幫助你放鬆，並且趕走壓力。

Sports also contribute to academic performance. Playing a sport requires a lot of time and energy; therefore, some people may think this would distract students from schoolwork. However, the opposite is true. Research has shown that children who participate in sports benefit intellectually and perform better in school. This is because exercise enhances

運動也幫助學業上的表現。做一項運動需要很多的時間和精力，因此，有些人可能想這會使學生的學業分心。然而，恰恰相反。研究顯示兒童參與運動對他們的智商和學業表現會更好。這是因為運動增強了幫助學習的特定心理過程。

development of specific mental processes which help study.

In a nutshell, sports and outdoor activities help develop many motor skills, confidence, academic performance, and teach people to love the natural world around them.

總而言之，運動跟戶外活動幫忙發展許多的動能技巧、自信、學業學習，而且教人們愛他們周圍的大自然。

關鍵單字解密

1. psychologically *adv.* 心理上地	2. coordination *n.* 協調
3. loosen *v.* 鬆開	

文法應用解析、深入應用補一補

❶ They are beneficial to your health in several ways.

解析

beneficial *adj.* 有益的。對某人是有益的這麼說："beneficial to 某人"，或："sth is beneficial"；以及用其動詞—benefit，慣用句型為："某人 benefit (from sth)"。

其它應用

The participation of children in team sports is beneficial in building teamwork skills and learning valuable social skills that can later be used in school and work.（孩子們在團隊運動中的參與，對建立團隊合作能力，和學習寶貴的社會技能是有益的，這些技能之後也可活用在學校和工作中。）

❷ Regarding emotional benefits, participating in sports and spending time outdoors helps you to loosen up and let go of stress.

解析

Regarding 無人稱獨立分詞構句，作為習慣用法，因其文法之複雜，只管它的意義已足夠。

其它應用

Regarding social benefits, participating in sports can help build relationships with peers and boost friendships.（關於健康上的效益，參加體育運動可以幫助建立與同伴的關係和提振友誼。）

7-2 全民運動

| 應用句型 |
A be composed of B.
A 由 B 組成

| 搭配口說主題 |
全民運動

重點文法搶先看

① 被動句的分詞構句

② 形容詞、副詞與對等子句的分詞構句

重要句型與文法放大鏡

① 被動句的分詞構句形成步驟如下：

1. 去連接詞（如：because／when）和副詞／形容詞子句中的主詞（二主詞相同時才能去）。
2. 若去掉的主詞是被執行該句的動作，副詞子句／形容詞中的一般動詞，去掉 be 動詞，留下過去分詞 Vpp。

例 1 形容詞子句 Baseball is the most popular sport **which is** played in my country.

→ 分詞構句 Baseball is the most popular sport **played** in my country.（棒球是我國最受歡迎的體育項目。）

例 2 副詞子句 Some people joke that KTV is the Taiwanese national sport **because they are obsessed by singing in a KTV studio**.

→ 分詞構句 **Obsessed by singing in a KTV studio**, some people joke that KTV is the Taiwanese national sport.（有人開玩笑説，KTV 是台灣的全民運動，因為它們為在 KTV 唱歌痴迷。）

例 3 對等子句 Baseball **was first introduced** during Japanese rule in the 1920s **and** it has become very popular since.

→ 分詞構句 **First introduced** during Japanese rule in the 1920s, it has become very popular since.（自棒球在 1920 年的日本統治期間首次引入，它已很受歡迎。）

文法和口說應用大結合

以上文法和句型可以運用到 IBT、NEW TOEIC 及 IELTS 考試上面，以下列的題目舉例 Track 32

What are the common sports played in your country?
什麼是貴國最常見的運動？

高分範文

Popular sports in Taiwan include baseball, basketball, and martial arts such as Tai Chi Chuan and Taekwondo, which are also practiced by many people. Speaking from my knowledge, I would say baseball is by far the most popular sport among these. It is generally regarded as the national sport in Taiwan. The official baseball league in Taiwan is the Chinese Professional Baseball League (CPBL), which is composed of

在台灣受歡迎的運動包括棒球、籃球、武術，如太極拳、跆拳道，也有很多人練。就我所知，我會説棒球是其中迄今為止最流行的運動。它通常被視為台灣的全民運動。大聯盟是中國職業棒球聯賽（中華職棒），由四支球隊組成。兄弟象，總部設在台北市，可能是最被看好的。在競技場觀看比賽是一個極好的

four teams. The Brother Elephants, based in Taipei City, are probably the most favored. Watching games in an arena is a fascinating cultural experience, where you can hear thunderous cheering.

文化體驗，在這裡你可以聽到雷鳴般整齊的歡呼。

Taiwan has been "exporting" a few of her brightest baseball talents to the top teams in Japan and United States over the past few decades, such as Chien-Ming Wang to the New York Yankees and then Washington Nationals.

在過去幾十年中，台灣已經"出口"了幾個最前途光明的棒球人才到日本和美國的頂級球隊，如王建民一先後效力於紐約洋基隊，然後是華盛頓國民隊。

It is undeniable that baseball is the national sport which is obsessed over by the majority of Taiwanese. However, after school, you can see many students playing basketball and

不可否認，棒球是全民運動，為多數的台灣人所痴迷。然而，放學後，你可以看到很多學生打籃球，學校開放田徑場給民眾跑步。此

people jogging along a school track when it is open for the public after school. Also, in the park, some people practice Tai Chi Chuan. It is rarely the case that you see citizens playing baseball.

外，在公園裡，有些人練太極拳。你很少會看到市民打棒球的情況。

關鍵單字解密

1. Tai Chi Chuan *n.* 太極拳	2. Taekwondo *n.* 跆拳道
3. arena *n.* 競技場	

文法應用解析、深入應用補一補

❶ It is generally regarded as the national sport in Taiwan.

解析

“be regarded as N.” 是「把……看作 N」，「把……認為 N」，可加形容詞：generally（一般）／unquestionably（毫無疑問）／definitely（絕對）regarded as... .,

其它應用

In Taiwan, Chien-Ming Wang is unquestionably

regarded as the most famous baseball star.（在台灣，王建民無疑算是最有名的棒球明星。）

❷ ... (CPBL), which is composed of four teams.

解析 A 由 B 組成 可用主動語態或被動語態。(CPBL) consists of four teams

大團體	小團體
主動語態：小團體組成大團體	被動語態：大團體由小團體組成。
小團體 comprise 大團體	大團體 be comprised of 小團體
小團體 compose 大團體	大團體 be composed of 小團體
小團體 constitute 大團體	大團體 be made up of 小團體
大團體 consist of 小團體	--

其它應用 1

Four teams compose the major league, CPBL.

或：Four teams constitute CPBL.（大聯盟是由四支球隊組成。）

其它應用 2

Baseball is a bat-and-ball game played between two teams; each team consists of nine players.

或：Each team is composed of nine players.（棒球是兩隊之間球棒和球的比賽；每個團隊由 9 名隊員組成。）

7-3 國內外旅遊和偏好

應用句型		搭配口說主題
Having said... 如前所述……		國內外旅遊和偏好

重點文法搶先看

① 進行式變化成分詞構句的用法

② 完成式變化成分詞構句的用法

③ Having said... = as I have said...／Having talked about... =. As/After we have talked about...

重要句型與文法放大鏡

① 副詞子句除了被動式（be＋Vpp），若為進行時（be＋V-ing），也省略 be 動詞，剩現在分詞 V-ing。

例 1 **While I was travelling** in Paris, I met some friendly and interesting people.省略 **While I was** 後 → **Travelling** in Paris, I met many friendly and interesting people.（當我在巴黎旅行時，我遇到了一些友善又有趣的人。）

② 完成式要改成分詞構句，將助動詞 has／have 改為 having 即可。

例 2 副詞子句 **After I have been to many countries,** I come to realize that my country is the most comfortable place to travel.

分詞構句 → **Having been to many countries**, I come to realize that my country is the most comfortable place to travel.（去過很多國家之後，我體會到，我國是旅遊的最舒服的地方。）

③ **Having said… 是 as I have said…的分詞構句；Having talked about… 是 As/After we have talked about…的分詞構句**

例：I prefer travelling abroad, and as I have said, this is only possible when I have time and money.

分詞構句 → Having said I prefer travelling abroad, this is only possible when I have time and money.（我更喜歡出國旅行，正如我剛才所説，這是當我有時間和金錢時才有可能的。）

 文法和口說應用大結合

以上文法和句型可以運用到 IBT、NEW TOEIC 及 IELTS 考試上面，以下列的題目舉例 Track 33

What do you suggest tourists do in your country?
你想建議來本國的遊客做些什麼？

 高分範文

Taiwan is a subtropical island full of attractions. I will introduce these attractions from the north to the south. Let me start from Taipei, our capital city. Taipei is a very vibrant and modern city so there are many things to see and do; for example, you can go to the most famous night markets where they sell a variety of street food. I recommend you visit National Chiang Kai-shek Memorial Hall, where it is well-worth watching the changing of the guards.

台灣是一個充滿景點的亞熱帶島嶼。我將從北到南介紹這些景點。讓我先從我們的首都 — 台北。台北是一個非常有活力的現代城市，所以有很多可以看和做的；例如，你可以去最有名的夜市，在那裡出售各種街頭食品。我建議您參觀中正紀念堂，那裡衛兵交接很值得看。

Heading south to mid-Taiwan, you can stop at some indigenous tribes' villages to experience their diverse cultures. You will admire their gift of singing. Going further to the south, I suggest you go to Kaohsiung, the second biggest city. You can go to the harbor to admire the beauty of the sea and enjoy fresh seafood.

南下到中台灣，你可以在一些原住民部落的村莊停下來，體驗他們不同的文化。你會佩服他們的歌唱天賦。進一步去南方，我建議你去第二個最大的城市，高雄。你可以去海港，欣賞大海的美景，享受新鮮的海鮮。

Next, Kenting is the most southern tourist town. It is amazingly beautiful. It is located in the south peninsula of Taiwan, standing out among the deep blue Pacific Ocean with green mountains in the middle. People engage in water activities, such as scuba diving, water scooter and sailing. In the evening, you cannot call it Taiwan without

接下來，最南端的旅遊小鎮——墾丁，它真的有令人讚嘆的美。它位於台灣南部的半島，矗立在深藍色的太平洋中，中間有綠色的山脈。人們從事水上活動，如潛水、水上摩托車和帆船。到了晚上，就不能不說一說台灣的美食，鎮中心到處是小

delicacies; the town center is filled with food stands and other marvellous goods for sale. Of course, the food will never let you down.

吃攤和其他有趣的雜貨。當然，食物永遠不會讓你失望。

關鍵單字解密

1. subtropical *adj.* 亞熱帶的	2. attractions *n.* 景點
3. vibrant *adj.* 有活力的	4. peninsula *n.* 半島
5. marvellous *adj.* 奇妙的	

文法應用解析、深入應用補一補

❶ Taiwan is a subtropical island full of attractions.

解析

表示充滿的片語有：“be full of... .”、“be filled with... .”、“be packed with...”。其中 full 是形容詞，fill 和 pack 是動詞，用被動語態。注意介系詞的不同。

其它應用

The two banks of the River Seine are full of local people and tourists; unpleasantly, the air is filled with the smell of vehicle emissions, cigarettes and even urine.（塞納河兩岸充滿了當地人和遊客，空氣中瀰漫著車輛廢氣、菸味，甚至尿味，讓人感到不悅。）

❷ It is well-worth watching the changing of the guards.

解析

表示值得的事物，可用名詞──“worth”表達，即：“be worth N/Ving”；或用其形容詞（adj.）── “worthy” 表達，即：“be worthy of N/Ving”；注意 worth 或 worthy, 有無用 “of” 的情況。

其它應用 1

Rome is a city（which is）worth visiting.（羅馬是值得一遊的城市。）

其它應用 2

Before you go to another country, I suggest you do some research on that destination. There are many people sharing their experiences and offering advice online. Some of them are worthy of being considered.（你到另一個國家之前，我建議你對那個目的地作一些研究。有許多人在網上分享他們的經驗，並提供建議。其中一些值得考慮。）

7-4 增加自行車專用道

｜應用句型｜
Before encouraging...
在鼓勵之前……

｜搭配口說主題｜
自行車專用道

重點文法搶先看

① 分詞構句和時間順序有關的連接詞

② 選擇簡化成分詞構句時，要注意原句是主動或是被動

重要句型與文法放大鏡

① 改成分詞構句時，需要留下連接詞的情形還有：與時間順序有關的連接詞：before、after、since。

例 **Before they encourage** citizens to cycle to work and school, local governments should build cycle lanes to ensure cyclists' safety.

分詞構句 → **Before encouraging** citizens to cycle to work and school, local governments should build cycle lanes to ensure cyclists' safety.（在鼓勵市民騎自行車上班和上學之前，地方政府應該建立自行車專用道，以確保騎

車人的安全。）* *此時 before **有必要保留，以顯出主要子句動作發生的時間早得多。**

② 簡化成分詞構句時，要注意原句是主動或是被動，要用對分詞 Ving 或 Vpp。副詞子句是主動，但**過去式**時，同學常忘掉使用主動的 Ving 時，因為以為是被動句：

例 After financial incentives **are provided** for companies to buy bikes for their employees to borrow for free, traffic will become less crowded and air will become cleaner.

分詞構句 → After financial incentives **provided** for companies to buy bikes for their employees to borrow for free, traffic will become less crowded and air will become cleaner.（在提供了企業購買自行車為員工免費借用的財政獎勵之後，交通流量將不那麼擁擠，空氣將會變得更乾淨。）→ **此句是被動**

例 1 After the city started to provide financial incentives for promoting cycling to work, the city has become tidier and cleaner.

分詞構句 → After starting to provide financial incentives for promoting cycling to work, the city has become tidier and cleaner.（在該市開始為推廣騎自行車上班，提供財政獎勵之後，該城市已變得更整潔和乾淨。）→ **此句是主動**

文法和口說應用大結合

以上文法和句型可以運用到 IBT、NEW TOEIC 及 IELTS 考試上面，以下列的題目舉例 Track 34

Many countries or cities have been promoting cycling to and fro work. However, not all people agree with the idea that some roads should be replaced with cycle lanes. What is your view on this? Give your reasons in details.

許多國家或城市一直在提倡騎自行車往返工作。然而，並不是所有的人都同意有道路應被替換為自行車道的想法。請問您對此有何看法？請詳述理由。

高分範文

I support the government's idea of encouraging people to cycle to and fro work. This behavior can benefit both individuals and the environment greatly. Taiwan is one of the top population **density** cities in the world. In order to help relieve already deteriorating traffic and

我支持政府鼓勵人民騎自行車上下班的想法，這同時提供給個人和環境諸多好處。台灣是世界密度最高的城市之一，人應要盡可能地騎自行車去上班，以幫助緩解已經惡化的交通，以及其引起的空氣

consequently air pollution, people should cycle to work as much as possible .Therefore, cycling now should have more functions than merely being a leisure sport.

污染。因此，現在騎自行車不僅僅是作為休閒運動，應該有更多的功能。

Before this can work, there should be some cycling infrastructures, such as cycle lanes or paths which only allow bikes; otherwise, it is not safe to cycle to work. However, there has been controversy about whether on-road cycle lanes make cyclists safer or put them in more tough situations. The problem lies in the fact that there are too many peripheral devices and regulations should be taken care of, such as good traffic light systems and roundabout designs and regulation on

在此之前，應該有一些騎自行車的基礎設施，如自行車道或路徑，只允許自行車；否則，騎自行車去工作是不安全的。然而，一直有爭議存在 — 在道路上的自行車道保護騎士保護，或其實是讓他們處在更艱難的情況下。問題在於有太多應採取的周邊設備和規定，如良好的交通燈、圓環的設計，和汽車濫用自行車道的管制。否則，增加或拓寬道路上的自行

automobiles abusing bikes. Otherwise, increasing or widening on-road cycle lanes can only put cyclists in more danger.

車道只會使騎自行車的人更危險。

關鍵單字解密

1. density *n.* 密度	2. leisure *n.* 休閒
3. controversy *n.* 爭議	4. peripheral *adj.* 周邊的

文法應用解析、深入應用補一補

❶ People should cycle to work as much as possible.

解析

表示盡可能多的句型："as much/many as possible"，many 指涉可數名詞；much 指涉不可數名詞。也可以用其他形容詞或副詞：as adj/adv as possible，表示盡……可能的。

其它應用 1

The relevant authorities should also provide safe security and covered cycle parking places as many as possible.（有關部門應盡可能提供安全保障和涵蓋自行車車位。）

其它應用 2

Some cities, such as Paris and Taipei provide bikes for people to borrow; to offer more incentives, the first half hour is for free in order to encourage people to use bikes as many as possible.（一些城市，如巴黎和台北，提供人們借用自行車；為提供更多的獎勵，前半個小時是免費的，以鼓勵人們盡可能多使用自行車。）

❷ However, there has been controversy about whether on-road cycle lanes make cyclists safer or put them in more tough situations.

解析

"There has been (much) controversy about/over ..." 表示一直存在著爭論、爭議。"controversy"是可數也是不可數名詞。

其它應用

There has been controversy about whether governments should set up on-road cycle lanes. People in Holland have witnessed that automobiles drive on already widened cycle lanes and this put cyclists in more hazardous situations.（一直存在有關政府是否應在道路上設立自行專用車道的爭議。在荷蘭，人們目睹了汽車駕駛開在已經拓寬的自行車道，這種行為使騎自行車更危險。）

7-5 增加自用車的稅金，進而減少自用車的使用量

｜應用句型｜
分詞構句修飾語、分詞構句的位置

｜搭配口說主題｜
增加自用車的稅金，減少自用車的使用量

重點文法搶先看

① 分詞構句的位置

重要句型與文法放大鏡

① **分詞構句**的位置：**分詞構句**經常放句首，以**強調**動作發生的**時間或原因**，但也可放句中主詞之後，或是句尾，且都要以逗號和主句隔開。**以下舉列：分詞構句中，否定字 not / never 要放在分詞前面。有些字本質上已具備了否定的意思，例如 never、nothing、nobody、nowhere、no one、seldom、hardly、scarcely、barely。**

例 1 Increasing the costs of driving can also cause unemployment for car manufacturers, **so it is not a panacea**. 分詞構句 → **Not a panacea**, increasing the costs of driving can also cause unemployment for car manufacturers.（開車成本的提升也可能導致汽車製造業的

失業，所以它不是萬靈丹。）

提點 分詞構句構造上似形容詞，所以要臨近與它最相關的部分。所以此例不放句尾，因 panacea 不是修飾 car manufacturers，要避免偏離句意。

例 2 **For people who live in remote areas**, they would feel very perturbed and regard it as unfair to be levied with more tax in order to discourage them from driving since public transport rarely reaches them.（對於住在偏遠地區的人來說，因為公共交通很少到達，向他們徵收更多的稅以勸阻不自駕車，他們會覺得很不安，認為這是不公平的。）

分詞構句 →

放句首 **Living in remote areas**, people would feel very perturbed and regard it as unfair to be levied with more tax in order to discourage them from driving. 提點 這裡 they 用 people 取代，否則不明白是誰。

放句中 People, **living in remote areas**, would feel very perturbed and regard it as unfair to be levied with more tax in order to discourage them from driving.

放句尾 People would feel very perturbed and regard it as unfair to be levied with more tax in order to discourage them from driving, **living in remote areas**.

提點 living in remote areas 不修飾 driving，所以不建議用此句。

文法和口說應用大結合

以上文法和句型可以運用到 IBT、NEW TOEIC 及 IELTS 考試上面，以下列的題目舉例 Track 35

Some people urge that taxes on buying and using cars should be reduced while others strongly suggest that governments should tax private car owners heavily in order to reduce the amount of cars on the roads. What are your views? Provide your reasons with details.

有人敦促對購買和使用汽車的稅收應該減少，而有人則強烈建議政府應以加重徵稅私家車主以減少道路上的汽車數量。你的看法是什麼？

高分範文

I am in favor of reducing traffic congestion and will be happy to see fewer vehicles on the roads so that air pollution can be reduced.

我贊成減少交通擁塞，並且將很高興地看到道路上的車輛減少，這樣的可以減緩空氣污染。

However, I am struggling with the idea of solving traffic

不過，我對私人車車主徵收高稅率以解決

issues by imposing high rate taxes for private motor vehicle owners. This may sound selfish: I like to have a car to take me everywhere in some situations in which driving is more convenient than taking public transport. But, I really don't feel like paying a lot. I definitely understand that imposing more taxes on buying and using private cars can absolutely discourage people from those actions; as a result, it can reduce traffic on the road and also air pollution.

交通問題的想法掙扎。這可能聽起來很自私：我想有一輛車開到想去的地方，而且在某些時候，開車比搭乘交通工作方便得多。但是，我真的不想付出很多。我絕對理解加重購買和使用私家車的稅，完全可以勸阻這些行動；其結果是，它可以減少道路的交通流量和空氣污染。

Although I am reluctant, at the same time, I know this idea has long-term effects on improving traffic and the environment. I hope someone can come up with a better idea.

雖然我很不情願，但同時，我知道這主意對改善交通和環境有長期的影響。我希望有人能想出更好的主意。為減少空氣污染的緣故，

For the sake of reducing air pollution, there should be alternatives to raising the cost of using cars. Recently, I learned that there are plans to put solar cars on the market and car models have been developed to minimize carbon emissions. If these models are also fuel efficient, it can encourage consumers to shift to them.

應該有提高使用汽車成本的替代方案。近日，我得知太陽能汽車有上市計劃，減少碳排放汽車的模型已有發展。如果這些模型也省油，它可以鼓勵消費者轉移消費它們。

關鍵單字解密

1. impose *v.* 設置、加	2. alternative *n.* 替代方案
3. minimize *v.* 減少	4. shift *v.* 轉移

文法應用解析、深入應用補一補

❶ Although I am reluctant, at the same time, I know this idea has long-term effects on improving traffic and the environment.

解析

at the same time、in the meanwhile（在同一時間；同時）或只用 "meanwhile"，語意上相當於 when、while 的副詞子句。

其它應用

However, it would be a long-term solution. Therefore, at the same time, people must complain.（不過，這將是一個長期的解決方式。因此，同時，人們一定會抱怨。）

❷ For the sake of reducing air pollution, there should be alternatives to raising the cost of using cars.

解析

"sake" 是理由；緣故；利益，所以 "for the sake of N/Ving" 就是為了……理由／緣故／利益而做……。

其它應用

For the sake of decreasing numbers of exclusive cars used, I think that it is a good idea to charge private car owners more in order to lessen private cars on the roads.（為了減少行駛道路的汽車數量，我認為向私家車主多收費，以減少在道路上的車輛，是一個好主意。）

7-6 限制觀光人數

｜應用句型｜
Had it not been for...
要不是……

｜搭配口說主題｜
限制觀光人數

重點文法搶先看

① **假設語氣未來式倒裝句**

② 慣用句——要不是

重要句型與文法放大鏡

假設語氣的獨立分詞結構：二子句主詞相同者，稱分詞構句；二子句主詞不同者，稱獨立分詞結構，子句中的主詞不能去，與事實相反的 If 子句可變為倒裝句型，**即把助動詞／be 提前**，並省略 if，其餘於部分保留不變。這裡同樣的主詞，仍兩個都保留。

① **假設語氣未來式倒裝**：假設語氣未來式中，一旦省略 if，就必須將助動詞 should 挪至句首。**句型公式：If＋主詞＋should＋原形動詞……, 主詞＋will/can/may/should＋原形動詞**

例 **If this idea should be carried out**, less fuel will be consumed by transportation and less pollution will be emitted.

→ **Should this idea be carried out**, less fuel will be consumed by transportation and less pollution will be emitted.（如果這一想法被執行，運輸將消耗較少燃料，並減少排放污染。）

② 慣用句——要不是

A. 與現在事實相反：**If it were not for＋N...**；

例 **If it were not for the disturbance** from too many tourists, animal habitats would not be affected.（要不是遊客干擾太多，動物棲息地不會受到影響。）

→也可以改成倒裝句：**Were it not for＋N...** .,

Were it not for disturbance from too many tourists, animal habitats would not be affected.

B. 與過去事實相反：**If it had not been for+ N...** .,

例 **If it had not been for** the environmentalists' strong appeals, the damages which tourism caused would have expanded more severely.（如果不是因為環保人士的強烈呼籲，旅遊業造成的損失會擴大得更嚴重。）

→也可以改成倒裝句：**Had it not been for＋N...** ,

Had it not been for the environmentalists' strong appeals, the damages which tourism caused would have expanded more severally.

 文法和口說應用大結合

以上文法和句型可以運用到 IBT、NEW TOEIC 及 IELTS 考試上面，以下列的題目舉例 Track 36

In recent years, people have been suggesting that there should be regulations on the number of tourists. What is your view on restricting the number of tourists at a particular time in a certain area?

近年來，人們一直建議應該管制旅遊者的數量。你對在一個時間內限制特定區域的遊客人數有何看法？

 高分範文

I am in line with this view that the number of tourists should be restricted. Since a long time ago, people have been aware that tourism contributes to the degradation of cultural assets, local as well as global issues of resource depletion and environmental degradation. The long-term effect of tourism is

我在這個觀點，與旅遊者的數量應限制的看法一致。自很久以前，人們已經意識到，旅遊業有助於文化遺產的退化、當地以及全球性資源枯竭和環境惡化的問題。旅遊業的長期影響是氣候變化和地球的死亡。不僅如此，旅

climate change and the death of the Earth. More than that, tourism also impacts significantly on local people, affecting their daily life. Besides, in some areas, tourism has disturbed animal habitats and resulted in the loss of biodiversity.

遊業也顯著影響了當地的人民，影響了他們的日常生活。此外，在一些地區，旅遊業已擾亂動物的棲息地，並導致生物多樣性的喪失。

Of course people enjoy travelling, I am not now suggesting that tourism should be forbidden; rather, here I am arguing that there should be regulations on the number of tourists at a particular time. Talking about such regulations, some may think of raising entrance fees. Following the supply-demand theory, surely this will work.

當然，人們喜歡旅行，我現在不是在建議旅遊業應該被禁止；相反，在這裡我主張應該規定一定時間內的遊客人數。談到這樣的規定，有些人可能會認為提高入場費。按照供需理論，想必這會起作用。

However, this may lead to a

然而，這可能會導

phenomenon that only the wealthy have the power to enjoy amazing places on the Earth. To avoid this, I propose that people register their visits in advance. I understand that this is definitely not convenient, especially for spur-of-moment travellers; however, considering the bigger picture, a little bit of planning ahead and waiting will avoid over-visitation and conserve the nature of beauty and heritage sites for the next generations.

致一種現象，即只有富人有享受地球上令人驚嘆的地方的權力。為了避免這種情況，我建議人們提前登記他們探訪。據我所知，這肯定是不方便，特別是對臨時起意的旅客；然而，考慮到大局，提前做計劃和一點點的等待，將避免過度探訪，且能為下一代養護自然之美和文物古蹟。

關鍵單字解密

1. be forbidden *ph.* 被禁止	2. spur-of-moment *adj.* 臨時起意的

文法應用解析、深入應用補一補

❶ I am in line with this view that the number of tourists....

解析

表示與……看法符合、一致，可用："in line with the view that..."、"in agreement with..."、"in keeping with..."

其它應用

I am in line with the view that governments should not put restrictions on the amount of tourists visiting their tourist sites.（我的看法是，政府不應該限制參觀他們的旅遊景點的遊客數量。）

❷ Considering the bigger picture, a little bit of planning ahead and waiting will avoid... generations.

解析

"the bigger picture"指的是某事的整個始末；某事物的完整視圖。"considering the bigger picture," 指「考慮到大局」。

其它應用

Considering the bigger picture, there is an absolute need to limit tourists in an effort to protect the negative impacts from tourism.（考慮到大局，限制遊客有絕對的必要，以努力避免旅遊業受到負面的衝擊。）

8-1

論工作與生活間的平衡

｜以下列的題目舉例｜

- **Do you think that there are too many holidays throughout the year or are there not enough?** 你認為一年當中有太多的假日還是假日不夠呢？
- **To have a challenging job or to have an easy job?** 要挑戰性的工作或是輕鬆的工作？（Ch6 6-2）
- **Mobile phones, technology vs face-to-face interaction** 手機、科技和面對面的交流（Ch5 5-6）
- **the pros and cons of making friends at work** 跟同事做朋友的優點和缺點（Ch5 5-4）

❶ **表示難題二選一的開頭語**：To V or not to V? That is the question.

解析 1 這是有一句著名的台詞── 威廉·莎士比亞的戲劇──哈姆雷特的開頭語而來的。“To be or not to be - That is the question.”“生存還是毀滅…”是“女修道院場景”中的獨白。後來世人把 “to be” 改成其他的動詞，來詼諧地應用這一名言。

應用 1 To have a challenging job or not to have a challenging job? That is the question. (Ch6 6-2)

（要有輕鬆的工作，還是不要？那是個問題。《節選自（Ch6 6-2）》）

❷ **陳述個人觀點的開頭語**：as far as 某人 be concerned

解析 2 "as far as 某人 be concerned" 是「以某人而言」；「就某人而言」；「就某人的觀點」。而"as far as 某事 be concerned" 是就「某事而言」；「某事有關的」；「至於」（見下文第 4 點）

應用 2.1 As far as I am concerned, leading an easy life is not my life goal. (Ch6 6-2)（就我個人而言，過著輕鬆的人生不是我的人生目標。《節選自（Ch6 6-2）》

應用 2.2 As far as I am concerned, we should have holidays once a month so people can spend more time with their family and friends and do something which we do only once in a while.（就我而言，我們應該每個星期都有假日，那麼人們就可以和他們的家人和朋友一起度過，並且做一些我們平常久久做一次的事情。）

❸ **用來添加你剛才所說的**：in fact, as a matter of fact

解析 3 in fact、as a matter of fact（事實上）用來添加更多的東西到你剛才所說的；或用來表示你不同意別人剛才所說的。

應用 3.1 You do not have to agree with everything that your co-workers say; in fact, different opinions can lead to healthy conversations and debates. (Ch5 5-4)
（你不必同意同事所說的每一件事；事實上，不同的意見可以引發健康的對話和辯論。《節選自（Ch6 5-4）》）

應用 3.2 As a matter of fact, working people often take this time to go shopping, travel or visit someone who lives further. Therefore, we should have more holidays to allow people to do such kinds of things.（事實上，工作的人通常會利用這一段時間去購物、旅遊和拜訪住在遠方的某人。因此，我們應該要有更多的假日，才可以去做這些事情。）

❹ **用來描述你正在討論的特定領域**：In terms of、as far as sth. is concerned

解析 4 In terms of、as far as sth. is concerned（在……的方面、至於）

應用 4.1 In regard to life goals, as far as I am concerned, leading an easy life is not my life goal. (Ch6 6-2)（至於生目標，就我個人而言，過著輕鬆的人生不是我的人生目標。）《適用於（Ch6 6-2）》）

應用 4.2 In terms of making time for family or friends, this is especially important for workers who need to work on holidays to enable people to shop in their stores or dine in their restaurants.（就為家人和朋友安排時間而言，這對於必須在假日工作的人格外的重要，他們使得一般人們假日能夠在他們的店裡購物，或是在他們的餐廳吃飯。）

應用 4.3 As far as the work load is concerned, if we come back to work after relaxing and recharging on holidays, we can work more efficiently.（就工作量而言，如果我們在假日後放鬆和充電之後返回工作職場，我們的工作可以變得更有效率。）

⑤ **歸納表示論述最重要的一點**：Most importantly; above all;

解析 5 最重要的是：“Most importantly”、“above all”；同樣的重要：“某事 is equally important” 或 “The equally important＋N. is that...”

應用 5.1 Most importantly, no matter what your preference is, at least devote your time and energy to work during working hours. (Ch6 6-2) 重要的是，不論你的偏好是什麼，至少你在工作時間能夠致力你的時間和精力在工作上。《節選自（Ch6 6-2）》

應用 5.2 The holidays that we have are not enough because everyone needs to spend time with family at least once a month. Above all, I think that the point of having holidays is celebrating them with your family. If you don't spend time once a month, you are going to lose the sense of what family is all about.（我們現在的假日不夠，因為每個人都需要至少一個月一次和家人相處。最重要的是，我認為假日的意義是和你的家人一起慶祝它們。假如你沒有一個月一次和你的家人相處，你就會失去家庭的意義感。）

⑥ 做最後一項論點時用語：Last but not least

解析 6 "Last but not least"：最後一點，但不是最不重要的一點

應用 6.1 In addition, be a team player... Last but not least, be humorous. (Ch5 5-5)
此外，成為團隊的一員……。最後一點，但不是最不重要的，要有幽默感。《節選自（Ch5 5-5）》

應用 6.2 Last but not least, people should know the balance between work and leisure, not to become a workaholic or a worker who always focuses too much on expecting holidays.（最後一點，但不是最不重要的，人人需要知道工作和休閒之間的平衡，不要成為一位工作狂，或是一直期待假日的員工。）

8-2 論健康與民生的平衡（以有機食物、基因工程食物為例）

| 以下列的題目舉例 |

· **What do you think about organic foods/genetically modified foods? Is this kind of food (Are these kinds of foods) popular in your country?** 你對於有機食物／基因改造食物的看法是什麼？這一類的食物在你的國家很流行嗎？

· **The common sports** 常見的運動（Ch7 7-2）

· **Cycle lanes** 自行車專用道（Ch7 7-4）

① **表示「從個人的知識或經驗來談」的重要句型為：**speaking from my knowledge /experience、speaking from my own experience、speaking from one's personal experience

解析 1 不同於引述從研究、文章等資料庫所得的信息，而是要表示訊息來源是從個人從知識或經驗，提及可信性，就能用這些句型。

應用 1.1 Speaking from my knowledge, I would say baseball is by far the most popular sport among these.（Ch7 7-2）（就我所知，我會說棒球是其中迄今為止最流行的運動。《節選自（Ch7 7-2）》）

應用 1.2 Speaking from my own experience, I feel I am more energetic when I have organic foods every day.（從我自己的經驗來說，我覺得當我每天都吃有機食品時，我更加精力充沛。）

❷ 談到某事物的特質或設計是在「什麼情況下是很理想的」實用片語：makes it ideal for...

解析 2 "A makes it ideal for B..." 表示「A 使得它非常適合 B」；「A 對 B 是很理想的」。

應用 2.1 Taiwan has its diverse landscapes and rolling mountains, and this makes it ideal for many cyclists.（此外，台灣有其不同的自然景觀和連綿的高山，這使得它非常適合騎自行車的人。《適用於（Ch7 7-2）》）

應用 2.2 Due to the fact that organic foods provide much more nutrition than conventional foods, this makes it ideal for people who prefer to have little food or cannot have much food for a meal.（基於有機食物提供更多營養的事實，這使得它們對偏好每餐吃很少的食物，或是無法吃很多食物的人是很理想的。）

❸ **表示不受任何某事實或執行的影響：**In spite of the fact that...、despite the fact that...

解析 3 雖然、儘管可以用介系詞片語加名詞："In spite of sth.";如果名詞要修飾，可以用 that 子句："In spite of the fact that⋯."（盡管事實如此⋯）。也可以用這一個字——despite; 或"despite the fact that⋯"（注意 despite 沒有用介系詞。）

應用 3.1 In spite of the fact that the most famous player-Wang has been traded, young, Taiwanese boys proudly wear his former jersey from his time pitching for the Yankees.（儘管事實上，最有名的王某雖已被交易，還是有台灣年輕人從他為美國人投球之後，就自豪地穿上他的前球衣。《適用於（Ch7 7-2）》

應用 3.1 Organic farming is carried without using chemicals in the fertilizers and pesticides, rather, with natural fertilizers and methods. In spite of the fact that organic foods are considered to be healthier and environment friendly than conventionally grown foods, many people cannot afford them.（有機耕種是使用沒有化學物的肥料和殺蟲劑，而以天然的肥料和方法來耕種。儘管事實是，有機食物被認為是比傳統法成長食物更健康和環

保的，很多人還是無法負擔它們。）

❹ **表示讓步的重要句型：**It is undeniable that... .

解析 4 It is undeniable that⋯.表示「不可否認地」，讓步的 that 子句。形容詞 “undeniable ” 是由動詞 “deny（否認）”來的。

應用 4.1 It is undeniable that baseball is the national sport which is obsessed over by the majority of Taiwanese. However,⋯.(Ch7 7-2)（不可否認，棒球是全民運動，為被多數的台灣人所痴迷。然而，⋯⋯《節選自（Ch7 7-2）》）

應用 4.2 It is undeniable that it is generally agreed that GM food is not inherently riskier to human health than conventional food. However, there have been ongoing concerns by the public related to food safety, regulation, labelling and environmental impacts.（不可否認地，雖然一般基改食物並不固有地比傳統的食物對人體健康的風險更多，然而，大眾擔心關於食物的安全、管制、標籤和環境的影響。）

❺ **表示論點的證據是來自自己的觀察的重要說法：**That is/was my observation、My observation is that... .

解析 5：你可以先描述你的論點、現況跟事實，然後再接著說："That was my observation"（這是我的觀察）；也可以把以上的事實、現況涵蓋在 observation 之後的 that 子句，形成："My observation is that⋯."。

應用 5.1 It is rarely the case that you see citizens playing baseball. That was my observation. (Ch7 7-2)
你很少會看到市民打棒球的情況。這是我的觀察。《適用於（Ch7 7-2）》）

應用 5.2 Although people claim that they cannot afford organic foods, my observation is that they spend a large amount of money on dining in very expensive restaurants.（雖然人們宣稱他們無法負擔有機食物，但我的觀察是，他們花很多的錢在很貴的餐廳用餐。）

❻ **表示罕見的、難得一見的：**this is rarely the case、be rarely seen

解析 6 類似上一個例子 5，你可以先描述你的論點、現況跟事實，然後再接著說："this is rarely the case"；也可以把以上的事實、現況涵蓋在 case 之後的 that 子句，形成："this is rarely the case that..."

應用 6.1 However,⋯.It is rarely the case that you see citizens playing baseball. (Ch7 7-2)（棒球是全民運動，為多數的台灣人所痴迷。然而，⋯⋯你很少會看到市民打棒球的情況。《節選自（Ch7 7-2）》）

應用 6.2 I am happy to see the price of organic foods going down and genetically modified foods disappear; this is rarely seen in Taiwan.（我很樂意見到有機食品的價錢下降，基因改造食品能夠消失；這情形在台灣是很罕見的。）

8-3 對交友之價值觀

｜以下列的題目舉例｜

- **Which do you think is more important in terms of friendship: quantity or quality?** 關於友誼，你認為是品質重要，還是數量比較重要？
- **Tell about how often you meet your friends and how you choose friends** 談多久和朋友見面與如何選擇朋友（Ch5 5-1）
- **Friendship and social activities** 友誼和社交活動（Ch5 5-2）
- **Friendship and social media** 友誼和社交媒體（Ch5 5-3）

❶ **表示某事對某人很重要的重要句型：**be very important to sb.、matter much、means a lot/significantly

解析 1 “Sth. be very important to 人”（某事對某人很重要）；也可以用 “matter”、“matter much”，或 “means”，如 “means a lot/significantly”。

應用 1.1 Friends are very important to me; therefore, I meet them as frequently as I can. (Ch5 5-1)（朋友對我來說非常重要；因此，我盡可能地經常跟他們見面。《節選自（Ch5 5-1）》）

應用 1.2 There are various kinds of "friends", ranging from people you know, you work with, to those you love like a sibling. However, what matters much more is how many of them are really close friends.（所謂的朋友，有各種各樣的，從你認識的人、和你一起工作的人、到你愛他們如同手足的人。然而，更重要的是，他們有多少是真正的親近的朋友。）

❷ **對於怎麼樣的朋友／人**：For friends/people who...

解析 2 "For people who…"（對於怎麼樣的人），也可以用 "those" 代替 "for those who…"，是關係子句，主格用 who，**受格**用 whom。

應用 2.1 For friends who have special shared hobbies or interests, they may organize regular activities, such as band practice, bowling matches, study groups, and so on. (Ch5 5-2)（對於有特殊共同的嗜好和興趣的朋友，他們可能會組織像是樂團練習、保齡球賽、讀書會等等活動。節選自（Ch5 5-2）》）

應用 2.2 For people who are your close friends, you know you can trust them, listen to their advice, and they do the same to you.（對於與你親近的朋友，你知道你可以信

賴他們、聽他們的建議，而他們也如此待你。）

③ 感官動詞的用法

解析 3 感官動詞是指跟五官功能或感覺有關的動詞，常見的感官動詞，有 see（看見）、watch（看見／監視）、observe（觀察到）、notice（注意到）、look at（注視）、hear（聽見）、listen to（傾聽，仔細聽）、smell（聞到）、taste、feel（感覺到）……，感官動詞是特殊的動詞，後面的第二個動詞（就是受詞補語）不接不定詞、它們接原形動詞，也可以接現在分詞（V-ing），但是它們語意上有些差別。如果受詞被動，用過去分詞（Vpp）。

應用 3.1 You can also see teenagers wandering around or hanging out aimlessly….(Ch5 5-2)（你也可以看見青少年在閒逛或是無目的消磨時光…《節選自（Ch5 5-2）》）

應用 3.1 Your real friend will listen to what you have to say. Moreover, when you get together, close friends usually speak your own language which no one else can understand.（你真正的朋友會仔細聽你說話。而且當你們在一起的時候，你們都會說些只有你們自己才懂的語言。）

❹ **表示儘管仍然的重要副詞：**nonetheless、nevertheless,

解析 4 Nonetheless、nevertheless 與 however 有時可以互換，都是用來表示想要第二點對比第一點。但 "however" 在意義上更接近「但是」；而 "Nonetheless" 接近「儘管」，也就是說，雖然有對比，但是仍然 有其好處（或壞處）。"nonetheless"等同 "nevertheless"，但 "nonetheless" 較正式。

應用 4 Nonetheless, I know people who are concerned about online privacy and safety. (Ch5 5-3)（然而，我知道一些人會擔心網路隱私和安全。《適用於（Ch5 5-3）》）

應用 4.1 Some people have many friends; nonetheless, a greater number of friends do not equal increased quality of social life.（一些人有許多的朋友，然而，有較多的朋友並不等於社交生活的品質提高。）

應用 4.2 To have a wide social collection is good; nevertheless, nothing can be compared with having truly good friends.（有很寬廣的社交集合是很好的；然而，沒有事情能夠比上有真正的好朋友。）

❺ **表示「是……而不是……」的重要連接詞**：rather than

解析 5 “rather than” 當連接詞時，意為「是……而不是……」我們常用 rather than 這個連結詞去加強其中重要性相對較高的事情。其前後所連接的兩個字，在詞性和結構上必須相稱。rather than 可作介系詞用（＝ instead of），表「而不是……」之意，句型為：Rather than＋ n / V-ing, …。

應用 5.1 Many people choose friends whose personality traits are similar to theirs rather than different from. (Ch5 5-1)（很多人選擇和自己相似，而非不同的個人特質當朋友。《適用於（Ch5 5-1）》）

應用 5.2 Rather than sharing your true feelings with everyone, you should distinguish who are your true friends from those who are distant friends.（你應該要會區分誰是你真正的朋友，和誰是要保持距離的朋友，而不是將你的真實感受和每個人分享。）**此句“rather than” 當介系詞。

❻ **表示總結的重要詞彙**：Anyway、all in all

解析 6 在思考、考慮之後的總結：Anyway、all in all（總而言之；言而總之）

應用 6.1 I don't choose friends based on their looks.... . Anyway, I don't make friends based on attractiveness. 我不基於外觀選擇朋友。總而言之，我交友不是看魅力的。(Ch5 5-1)《適用於（Ch5 5-1）》

應用 6.2 All in all, nothing is better than true friends who know everything about you and always support you. Stay away from "sunny day" friends.（總而言之，沒有任何事情能夠比得上真正的朋友，他們知道你的所有事情，並且總是支持你。遠離酒肉朋友。）

8-4 稅和社會福利

｜以下列的題目舉例｜

- **A nation's welfare usually comes from their people's income taxes. Do you prefer to pay more taxes in order to receive more social welfare, or the opposite is true?** 一個國家的福利通常來自於人民的所得稅。你偏好交更多稅以換取更好的社會福利，還是相反呢？
- **The impact of tourism on the environment** 觀光對於環境的影響（Ch6 6-4）
- **Cycle lanes** 自行車專用道（Ch7 7-4）
- **Playing sports/outdoor activities** 運動／戶外活動（Ch7 7-1）
- **The common sports** 常見的運動（Ch7 7-2）
- **Views on taxing private car owners heavily** 對加重徵稅私家車的看法（Ch7 7-5）

❶ **用來舉例的重要片語：** Take sth for example、Another example is...

解析 1 "Take sb./sth for example"（以某人某事為例）、"Another example is…"（另外一個例子是）。

應用 1.1 Take CO2 emissions for example, this release consequently results in acid rain, global warming and photochemical pollution. (Ch6 6-4)（以二氧化碳排放量為例，排放的結果導致酸雨，全球暖化和光化學污染。《適用於（Ch6 6-4）》）

應用 1.2 Another example is Scandinavian countries that raise large amounts of tax revenue for redistribution and social insurance while maintaining some of the strongest economic outcomes in the world.（另外一個例子是北歐四國，他們徵很大量的稅收，用來重新分配與社會保險，同時也在世界上維持者很強大的經濟結果。）

❷ **用以傳達偏好的重要片語：**be in favor of、prefer A to B

解析 2 "be in favor of＋Ving"（贊成）、"prefer A to B"（愛 A 多於 B）

應用 2.1 I am in favor of reducing traffic congestion and will be happy to see fewer vehicles on the roads so that air pollution can be reduced. (Ch7 7-5)（我贊成減少交通擁塞，並且將高興地看到在道路上的車輛較少，這樣的空氣污染可以減少。《節選自（Ch7 7-5）》

應用 2.2 From these successful examples, I would like to pay more to get my retirement covered; that is to say, I am in favor of higher taxes for social welfare.（從這些成功的例子，我願意付更多以照顧我的退休。也就是說，我贊成為社會福利收較高的稅。）

③ **表示「不僅、還有、此外」的另一種選擇：** Not only that,...

解析 3 表達「不僅、還有、此外」除了用："And what is more"、"furthermore"、"aside from"、"besides that"、"moreover"，還有 "Not only that"（不只是那樣；不僅如此）

應用 3.1 Not only that, they can also help you psychologically. (Ch7 7-1)（不僅如此，它們也可以有心理上的幫助。《適用於（Ch7 7-1）》）

應用 3.2 Not only that, I especially don't like the government using my hard-earned money to support some people who don't like to work.（不只是那樣，我特別不喜歡政府使用我的辛苦錢來支持一些不工作的人。）

④ **表示罕見的／常有的事：** as is rarely/often the case

解析 4 "It is rarely the case"、"as is rarely the case"（這是罕見的事）。"case" 可以＋that 子句。"It is often the case"、"as is often the case"（這是常有的事。）**提點**

“as”是連接詞。

應用 4.1 It is rarely the case that you see citizens playing baseball.(Ch7 7-2)（你很少會看到市民打棒球的情況。《節選自（Ch7 7-4）》）

應用 4.2 In Taiwan, we pay much less income taxes and consumer taxes than these successful European countries in terms of social welfares. However, as is often the case, our citizens complain that our social welfares are far inferior to those countries.（在台灣，我們繳納所得稅和消費稅比這些在社會福利上成功的歐洲國家要少得多。然而，我們的市民常常抱怨說，我們的社會福利都遠不如這些國家，是常有的事。）

⑤ **表「目的」的副詞子句**：so that、for the purpose that...、to the end that...

解析 5 **表「目的」的副詞子句**有：“so that”、“for the purpose that”，或 “to the end that”。“so that” 和 “so as to” 可以互換。

應用 5.1 I will be happy to see fewer vehicles on the roads so that air pollution can be reduced. (Ch7 7-5)

（我將很高興地看到在道路上的車輛減少，這樣的可以減緩空氣污染。《節選自（Ch7 7-5）》）

應用 5.2 I would rather let the government take more money so that we will have better pension.
= I would rather let the government take more money so as to have better pension later.（我寧願讓政府拿更多的錢，以便以後能有更好的養老金。）

❻ **表示結論的片語：**in a nutshell、in summary、in short、in brief

解析 6 做歸納結論可用 “in a nutshell”、“in summary”（簡而言之）。還有之前介紹過的：“in short”、“in brief”。“nutshell”（堅果的外殼），是小的東西，所以意思很明顯，也就是將長篇大論用一句話總結的意思。

應用 6.1 In a nutshell, sports and outdoor activities help develop many motor skills, confidence, academic performance, and teach people to love the natural world around them. (Ch7 7-1)（總而言之，運動跟戶外活動幫忙發展許多的動能技巧、自信、學業學習，而且教人們愛他們周圍的大自然。《節選自（Ch7 7-1）》

應用 6.2 In a nut shell, there is an old saying, men propose; God disposes. The nation is much stronger than any individual; well, at least, it is the case in my country.（簡而言之，有一句老諺語：謀事在人，成事在天。國家比任何個體都強大很多；至少在我的國家是如此。）

8-5

商業化的節日

｜以下列的題目舉例｜

- **Do you think holidays have become too commercialized? Tell your views with supporting detailed.**您認為假日已經變得太商業化？提供細節以支持你的看法。
- **Playing sports/outdoor activities** 運動／戶外活動（Ch7 7-1）
- **Views on the idea of global villages** 對地球村概念的看法（Ch6 6-5）
- **Cycle lanes** 自行車專用道（Ch7 7-4）
- **Views on taxing private car owners heavily** 對加重徵稅私家車的看法（Ch7 7-5）

❶ **用於給第一個重要原因：**To begin with, First of all,

解析 1 "To begin with,"、"First of all,"（首先；第一）

應用 1.1 To begin with, sports help you keep healthy physically and psychologically.（Ch7 7-1）（首先，運動幫助你保持身體上和心理上的健康。《節選自（Ch7 7-1）》）

應用 1.2 No, I don't think so. First of all, I feel good to receive presents.（不，我不這麼認為。首先，收禮物我覺得很開心。）

❷ 表示「以……的觀點來說；以……的角度來看」的重要片語：Talking from... perspective; speaking from... . perspective

解析 2 "Talking from …. perspective,"（以……的觀點來說；以……的角度來看）相同於之前介紹過的："speaking from …. perspective" 或 "speaking from perspective of…"。

應用 2.1 Talking from the perspective of economic benefits, take the European Union or EU for example, they have a unified currency, which is the Euro, and this makes business easier.(Ch6 6-5)（從經濟利益的角度來看，以歐盟也就 EU 是作為例子，他們有統一的貨幣，也就是歐元，使得商業活動更容易。《節選自（Ch6 6-5）》

應用 2.2 Talking from a child's perspective, they are happy to receive presents.（以小孩子的角度來看，他們很樂意接受禮物。）

③ 表示問題／原因存在於以下的事實：The problem/the reason lies in the fact that...

解析 3 “The problem/the reason lies in the fact that⋯.” 問題／原因存在於⋯⋯。

應用 3.1 The problem lies in the fact that there are too many peripheral devices and regulations should be taken care of, such as good traffic light systems and roundabout designs and regulation on automobiles abusing bikes. (Ch7 7-4)（問題在於有太多應採取的周邊設備和規定，如良好的交通燈、圓環的設計，和汽車濫用自行車道的管制。《節選自（Ch7 7-4）》）

應用 3.2 The reason lies in the fact that commercialized holidays obscure the focus of what holidays really mean; take Christmas for example, some people appear to focus more on what to buy and what they may receive than the birth of the savior, Jesus Christ.（事實是這樣的：商業化的假日模糊了假日實際意義的焦點。以聖誕節為例，一些人們明顯得更聚焦於要買什麼，和他們可以得到什麼，多於救世主基督——耶穌的誕生。）

④ **表示當一件事情發生時，別的事情也正在發生所用的重要片語**：at the same time、meanwhile,

解析 4 用 “meanwhile”、“at the same time”（同時）表示當一件事情發生時，別的事情也正在發生。

應用 4.1 Although I am reluctant, at the same time, I know this idea has long-term effects on improving traffic and the environment. (Ch7 7-5)（雖然我很不情願，但同時，我知道這主意對改善交通和環境有長期的影響。《節選自（Ch7 7-5）》）

應用 4.2 Meanwhile, I am cheered up and feel refreshed. Holidays are also the time when we show our appreciation to our parents as well. We buy them gifts too. It is a time of giving even though it's commercialized.（同時，我高興起來，感覺神清氣爽。假日通常也是我們顯示我們對父母的感激的時候。我們也買禮物給他們。這是給予的時刻，即使它是商業化的。）

⑤ **用來表示之前提的事是與事實完全相反的，或否認之前別人所說的看法**：However, the opposite is true。

解析 5 “opposite” 是名詞、形容詞、介系詞、也是副詞，都是相反的、對立的意思。所以 “the opposite is true” 意思是——反面才是真的；不是這一回事。

應用 5.1 Playing a sport requires a lot of time and energy; therefore, some people may think this would distract students from schoolwork. However, the opposite is true. (Ch7 7-1)（做一項運動需要很多的時間和精力，因此，有些人可能想這會使學生的學業分心。然而，恰恰相反。《節選自（Ch7 7-1）》）

應用 5.2 People now have reached a stage where they expect presents. It is often the case that we think we buy things which our family or friends like or want. However, the opposite is true.（人們現在已經到達了一個期待禮物的階段。但一般來說，我們認為我們買的東西是我們的家人和朋友喜歡的或是想要的。然而不是這一回事。）

❻ 做總結的其他用語：in a word、in a few words

解析 6 之前介紹的"In a nutshell"也可以用 "in a word"；"in few words"（總結一句；以一句話總結）這兩個片語代替；雖然是用 "a word"，但是是用一句話回答。

應用 6.1 In a nutshell, sports and outdoor activities help develop many motor skills, confidence, academic performance, and teach people to love the natural world around them. (Ch7 7-1)（總而言之，運動跟戶外活動幫忙發展許多的動能技巧、自信、學業學習，而且教人們愛他們周圍的大自然《節選自 (Ch7 7-1)》）

應用 6.2 In a few words, too much emphasis on gifts for holidays not only puts stress on people, but also creates an environment for children to grow up in a materialistic society.（總結一句，假日強調太多在禮物上面，不僅是加壓力於人們之上，也創造了一個使兒童在物質社會成長的環境。）

8-6 論媒體與社交（以談名人、寧作名人或是普通人為例）

| 以下列的題目舉例 |

· **What would you rather be, a famous person or an ordinary one?** 你寧願當名人或是平凡人？

· **Technology vs face-to-face interactions** 科技與面對面互動（Ch5 5-6）

· **While Mobile phone-based and web-based communication tools appear to play a significant role in people's daily lives, some argue that they have replaced face-to-face interaction with people. What is your opinion on this?** 手機和網路為基礎的溝通工具顯然在人們的日常生活中扮演重要的角色。然而，一些人爭論説社交媒體已經取代了人們面對面的交流。你認為呢？（Ch5 5-6）

· **Friendship and social activities** 交友和社交活動（Ch5 5-2）

· **Friendship and social media** 交友和社群媒體（Ch5 5-3）

❶ **回答是的其他回答法有：**Yes, indeed、yes, that's true

解析 1 "Yes, indeed"（是的，的確是）；"Yes, that's true"（是的，的確是）

應用 1.1 Yes, indeed, the technology in developing mobile phone-based and web-based communication tools has been greatly enhanced. (Ch5 5-6)（是的，的

確，在發展手機和網路為基礎的溝通工具的科技已經進步很多。《節選自（Ch5 5-6）》）

應用 1.2 Yes, indeed, I would like to be a somebody. I think many people really have a desire to be a famous person who is liked and admired by others.（是的，的確是，我想要做大人物。我是認為很多人真的有慾望要成為有名的人，受到別人喜愛與欣賞。）

❷ **強調某事是真實的、的確的其他方式：**It is true that、actually、literally

解析 2 "It is true that＋子句"、"actually"、"literally" 都表示是真實的。"literally"（從字面上）副詞，用於顯示你說的是真的，而不誇張。

應用 2.1 Yes, it is true that there are definitely some rules to keep in mind in the workplace. (Ch5 5-5)（是的，的確在工作場所有一些準則要牢記在心的。《節選自（Ch5 5-5）》）

應用 2.2 Also, it is true that with fame, power and wealth consequently become easier to get.（而且，就是真的有了名聲後，權力和財富也會接踵而來。）

❸ **用來表示是一直觀察到的現象：**As has been seen,

解析 3 “As has been seen”是完成式的句型，也可以用主動語氣表示：“as we have seen that⋯.”。

應用 3.1 As has been seen, these tools certainly have changed the way people interact. (Ch5 5-6)（已經可以見到的，這些工具確實已經改變人類交流的方式。《節選自（Ch5 5-6）》）

應用 3.2 As has been seen in some examples, some ordinary people who become famous, are invited to TV shows or to appear in commercial advertisements.（如同一直在一些例子所見，一些平常的人變得有名之後，他們會被電視節目所邀請，或是出現在商業廣告上。）

❹ **表示「雖然、儘管」的另外一種說法：**Having said⋯.

解析 4 此 “Having said⋯”「雖然、儘管」是只針對你自己的話，表示這是一個信號，預告你現在要說的，是跟剛剛所說的事情是相對立的。如果你只是要表達 —「就我剛剛所說的」就用 “As I have said,”。

應用 4.1 Having said their advantages, they also come with negative impacts. Many people unduly rely on these virtual tools and neglect real time being with friends and family. (Ch5 5-6)（已經談了它們的優點，它們也伴隨者負面的影響。很多人過度依賴這些虛擬的工具，然後忽略和他們朋友和家人真正相處的時間。《適用於（Ch5 5-6）》）

應用 4.2 Having said that I would rather be a celebrity, imagine that, if you are seeing someone, the news will spread. What will be the consequences if that relationship does not work out? Ordinary people can choose not to reveal their past relationships, but it is not the case for a celebrity.（雖然我說我寧願成為名人，但是想像，假如你和某人交往，媒體就會散播這件事。假如這段感情不成功，將會有什麼後果呢？一般人可以選擇不透露他們過去的情史。但是對名人而言，這是不可能的。）

⑤ 表示「結論是」的其他說法： to summarize、to sum up

解析 5 ："to summarize"、" to sum up"是表目的的不定詞（to-V）片語，意思是結論是……

應用 5.1 To summarize, I filter friends, choose who can see my news and pictures to protect myself and also allow my real friends to keep each other updated. (Ch5

5-3)（結論是，我過濾朋友、選擇誰可以看到我的動態和照片，以保護我自己，也允許我真正的朋友彼此更新現況。《節選自（Ch5 5-3）》）

應用 5.2 To summarize, being a celebrity can bring you power, attention and respect.（結論是，成為一名名人，可以帶給你權力、關注和尊敬。）

應用 5.3 To sum up, being a somebody puts you out in the forefront of public life, not behind it. They lose freedom in many ways. Therefore, I am happy to be an ordinary person.（總結是，成為一位大人物意味著你的生活會攤開在公眾面前，沒辦法藏著。他們在很多方面失去自由。因此，我很樂意作為一名平凡人。）

❻ **無論如何（**no matter**）加名詞子句**： no matter what... , no matter how

解析 6 no matter 可接不同的疑問詞成為名詞子句：no matter who（無論是誰）、no matter how much（無論多少）、no matter where（無論在哪）等。

應用 6.1 To summarize, no matter what we do, keeping each other company regularly is important to maintain friendships.(Ch5 5-2)（總之，不論我們做什麼，定期陪伴彼此，對於維持友誼很重要的。《節選自（Ch5 5-2）》）

應用 6.2 No matter what fame and how much wealth becoming a celebrity can bring, I would rather not expose myself under the spotlight, and become the topic of people's gossip.（不論成為名人可帶來名聲和多少的財富，我寧願不要把我自己暴露在鎂光燈之下，並且成為別人閒聊八卦的話題。）

考用英語系列 002

「聽」懂英文文法和長難句口語表達：應戰 iBT、New TOEIC、IELTS （附 MP3）

作　　者　陳儀眉 Tina
發 行 人　周瑞德
執行總監　齊心瑀
行銷經理　楊景輝
企劃編輯　饒美君
封面構成　高鍾琪

內頁構成　菩薩蠻數位文化有限公司
印　　製　大亞彩色印刷製版股份有限公司
初　　版　2017 年 7 月
定　　價　新台幣 399 元
出　　版　倍斯特出版事業有限公司
電　　話　(02) 2351-2007
傳　　真　(02) 2351-0887
地　　址　100 台北市中正區福州街 1 號 10 樓之 2
E-mail　best.books.service@gmail.com
網　　址　www.bestbookstw.com

港澳地區總經銷　泛華發行代理有限公司
地　　址　香港新界將軍澳工業邨駿昌街 7 號 2 樓
電　　話　(852) 2798-2323
傳　　真　(852) 2796-5471

國家圖書館出版品預行編目資料

「聽」懂英文文法和長難句口語表達 ： 應戰 iBT、New TOEIC、IELTS / 陳儀眉著. -- 初版. -- 臺北市 ： 倍斯特, 2017.07 面 ；　公分. --（考用英語系列 ； 2）
ISBN 978-986-93766-7-9（平裝附光碟片）
1.英語 2.語法
805.16　　105025552